"Can you k̶ ̶ ̶ ̶ ̶ ̶ ̶ ̶ ̶ ̶ ̶ped it in your ̶ ̶"

The blood roar̶ ̶ ̶ ̶

"Would you…sh̶ow̶ ̶m̶e̶?

Jack turned away to set his glass on the coffee table. Then he took Krysta's goblet from her unresisting fingers and put it beside his before turning to her. His hands shook slightly as he cupped her face with both hands, but the sensation of her warm skin beneath his fingers steadied him. He wanted nothing more than to kiss her the way she was meant to be kissed.

"Close your eyes," he murmured, gazing down at her as heat slowly flickered in his belly. "Close your eyes, and empty your mind of everything but this."

With a little sigh, she allowed her eyes to drift closed.

"Happy Valentine's Day," he whispered, just before his lips touched hers and their bodies melded.

Vicki Lewis Thompson has always admired the men brave enough to tackle writing a romance novel. Everybody knows guys don't understand that stuff, right? Wrong. Some have an incredible grasp on what makes a woman tick. These intrepid pioneers inspired Vicki to create Jack Killigan, a man who understands romance so well, he gave the author goose bumps.

Mr. Valentine is a special book for Vicki in many ways. Not only is the premise—and the hero— dear to her heart, but it also marks her 25th book for Temptation. Be sure to watch for Vicki's next 25 exciting books, available from Temptation and Love & Laughter.

Books by Vicki Lewis Thompson

HARLEQUIN TEMPTATION
555—THE TRAILBLAZER
559—THE DRIFTER
563—THE LAWMAN
600—HOLDING OUT FOR A HERO

HARLEQUIN LOVE & LAUGHTER
5—STUCK WITH YOU

Don't miss any of our special offers. Write to us at the following address for information on our newest releases.

Harlequin Reader Service
U.S.: 3010 Walden Ave., P.O. Box 1325, Buffalo, NY 14269
Canadian: P.O. Box 609, Fort Erie, Ont. L2A 5X3

Vicki Lewis Thompson
MR. VALENTINE

Harlequin Books

TORONTO • NEW YORK • LONDON
AMSTERDAM • PARIS • SYDNEY • HAMBURG
STOCKHOLM • ATHENS • TOKYO • MILAN
MADRID • WARSAW • BUDAPEST • AUCKLAND

With gratitude to Ed Hoornaert and Donna Lepley
for inspiring this story

And to all the unsung heroes laboring behind
female pseudonyms in the romance industry
Will you be my valentine?

ISBN 0-373-25724-4

MR. VALENTINE

Copyright © 1997 by Vicki Lewis Thompson.

1

"WELL, CAT, I HOPE to hell this is sexy enough."

From her basket next to the computer, a butterscotch tabby watched with an unblinking stare as Jack Killigan packaged up the romance novel he'd just written.

"Had to go back into the old memory bank," Jack continued, "considering it's been a while since I've had any hands-on experience." He scratched behind the cat's ears and looked into her green eyes as she began to purr. "But if you'll pardon me for bragging, I make damn good love on paper. Damn good."

He smoothed the label onto the envelope, running his fingers across the pseudonym he'd chosen for the project. *Candace Johnson*. Although Manchester Publishing had invited any unpublished novelist to enter a manuscript in its Valentine's Day romance contest, Jack firmly believed a woman stood a better chance than a man.

A chilly dawn forced its way through the drizzle of another November day on Puget Sound. He had just enough time to climb into his coveralls and rain gear, make the wet motorcycle trip to Rainier Paper and clock in at the shipping dock at eight. He'd mail the manuscript on the way.

Krysta would chew his butt again all through lunch about not getting enough sleep. He took off his glasses to massage the bridge of his nose. Then he put them back on and smiled. He doubted that she knew how much he enjoyed the self-improvement lectures she delivered on a regular basis while they shared a lunch table in the company cafeteria. Or how much she'd inspired this latest book.

KRYSTA LUECKENHOFF WALKED into the contracts office of Rainier Paper at ten minutes before eight, the first one in the office, as always. She started coffee perking, turned on her computer and straightened the papers on her already neat desk in an effort to quiet the turmoil in her mind. The routine refused to comfort her today. She'd planned so carefully, yet nothing was working out the way she'd hoped. It looked as if she wouldn't be able to afford live-in help for her father in September, after all.

She picked up a framed picture on her desk and brushed a speck of lint from the glass. She'd taken the snapshot the previous June, when all four of her younger brothers had managed to get the day off from their summer jobs to celebrate Father's Day. They'd had a picnic on the beach, her dad's favorite place to eat, and for the picture his sons had lifted him out of the hated wheelchair and propped him against a large piece of driftwood. Then they'd clustered around him, their young, strong bodies obscuring his wasted legs, and for the first time in years, Krysta had caught a glimpse, through the camera lens, of the man her father used to be.

Krysta put the picture down with a guilty start as Rosie Collins came into the office shaking rain from her umbrella.

"Hi, there," Krysta said, flashing a smile.

"Don't put on that fake grin for me." The dark-skinned brunette had become Krysta's friend in the two years they'd worked together in the contracts department. "When I first came in, there was tragedy all over that pretty face. Something's wrong."

Krysta sighed. "After you left last night Juliet called me in and told me she won't accept the vice presidency even if they offer it to her."

Rosie gazed at her with compassion. "Sorry, girl."

"Yeah. That means there's no promotion for Krysta, either." Krysta ran her fingers through her hair. "I can't blame her. She's decided to adopt a child and doesn't want the added responsibility."

"No kidding?" Rosie took a mug from her desk drawer and walked over to pour herself some coffee. "Bancroft's adopting a kid? That's a shocker."

"A little girl from China, no less. It's a very humanitarian thing to do, and you have to admire her for it, but I was so sure she'd accept the vice presidency and I'd get her job. And her paycheck."

"Listen." Rosie walked around behind Krysta's desk and gestured toward the picture of her family. "Ask those guys to help pay for your dad's live-in help. I never thought it was right that you're taking on the whole responsibility in the first place."

"They can't, Rosie. Not and keep going to school, and that's so much more important. Maybe if I request a transfer to marketing, I'll have a better shot at a promotion."

Rosie shook her head. "All this jockeying for position makes my head spin. It wouldn't kill your brothers to sit out a year and—"

"It would kill me. Once out, they might never go back. And education is the key. They have to finish."

"Okay, Mother Teresa." Rosie squeezed Krysta's shoulder and headed back to her desk. "I hope all these guys you're shepherding along appreciate you."

JACK CARRIED HIS TRAY over to the corner table where he and Krysta usually ate and waited while she hung her purse over her chair and took a seat before he settled down himself.

Krysta cast a quick glance over Jack's tray. "Coffee and carrot cake. My good friend, I hope that's not all you're having for lunch."

"Doesn't carrot cake count as a veggie?" He nudged his glasses back into position. He really had to get the broken earpiece fixed one of these days. Tape wasn't working worth a damn.

"No, carrot cake does *not* count as a veggie." She positioned her napkin in her lap before giving him a little smile. "Which you very well know."

He gestured toward his tray. "Actually, this isn't all I'm having."

"Thank goodness for that. A salad would be a very good idea, Jack." She took a dainty bite of hers, a concoction full of things like sprouts and fresh spinach.

"I was thinking in terms of three more cups of coffee. It's made from beans, isn't it?"

Krysta laughed and shook her head, causing her hair to ripple and glint like antique gold under the cafeteria's fluorescent lights. "You're a hopeless case. Clever but hopeless. You need the coffee because you spent another night in front of the tube, I'll bet."

"I did." It wasn't a lie, exactly. Computer monitors

and television sets were similar, and he wasn't about to tell anyone about his writing until he'd sold something. He felt more hopeful about that today than he had in a long time. Even he had to admit that his mysteries had been clueless, his horror too tame and his science fiction was on a technical level with Tinkertoys.

"Jack, you have such potential." Krysta dabbed at the corner of her mouth with her napkin. "You may not appreciate my bringing this up, but in high school you pulled down a B average, despite all the partying."

"Maybe it was *because* of the partying. The grindstone doesn't rub everyone the right way, you know."

"I worked in the school office. I happened to see your SAT scores. Ninety-ninth percentile, Jack. You should be making better use of your brain than muscling paper bales by day and sitting in front of the television by night."

"That sounds like a line from my parents, if ever I heard one."

Her expression turned adorably serious. "If I repeat what your parents say, it's because I happen to agree with them." She put a hand on his arm. "Look, I know it will be hard to go back to college again after so many years, but education is extremely important. Don't you realize your innate intelligence will atrophy if you don't use it?"

He knew he shouldn't tease her, but he couldn't seem to help himself. "I subscribe to *Motorcycle Mania.* Some of the articles are pretty good." He grabbed a napkin as a sneeze took him by surprise.

"That's another thing. You get no sleep and then you ride around in the rain on that big old Harley of yours, catching colds." She reached down and dug around in her purse. "Take these," she said, shoving a bottle of vitamin C tablets in his hand.

"No. They're yours." He set them back in front of her tray.

"Please take them. I'll pick up some more, but I know you won't. Maybe that bottle will get you through the worst of the rainy season, although I wish you'd consider buying a car. I'm sure you could qualify for a loan."

"Why would I want a car? They use more gas than my bike."

She rolled her eyes. "Because," she said with elaborate care, as if talking to someone of marginal intelligence, "no one will think of you as executive material if you hang on to that motorcycle. And you could use a good haircut. The shaggy look is out, Jack. I honestly wonder what you're spending your money on. I hope it's not something obnoxious like calling those nine-hundred numbers." She wrinkled her nose in obvious distaste.

He couldn't help laughing at her suggestion that he might be interested in phone sex. "No, I don't call nine-hundred numbers." He didn't tell her that he'd sunk all his spare cash into the best computer and printer he could find, because then she'd want to know why.

"Then what's your secret passion?" Fortunately she didn't pause for an answer. "I suppose you have one of those sound systems that drives the neighbors crazy." She took a drink of her mineral water and set the glass down with a decisive click. "Night school, Jack. That's the way to get ahead. My management class was invaluable, and now the public speaking class is a perfect complement. Do you have a catalogue from Evergreen Community College?"

"No."

"I'll get you one. The fall semester is half over, of course, but you could certainly enroll for the spring. You really need to rev up the motors on that brain of yours."

"You seem more into this improvement business today than usual. Did you get another set of instructions from the folks back home telling you to work harder on reforming me?"

A hint of vulnerability flashed in her eyes, then was gone. "No, no, I didn't."

"Something's eating you." He paused. She always prided herself on being upbeat and in charge, a walking advertisement for the power of positive thinking. That brief glimpse of a chink in her armor was unsettling. "Is it something about your father?" Last Jack had heard, Hans Lueckenhoff had been forced by weakening leg muscles into using a wheelchair. Maybe his condition had deteriorated even more.

"Everything's fine, really," Krysta said, looking deliberately cheerful. I—" Her gaze slid over his shoulder and up. "Oh, hello, Derek."

Jack grimaced. Derek Hamilton, the youngest vice president in the history of Rainier Paper, was apparently standing right behind him. Jack could guess why Hamilton was lurking around the company cafeteria instead of spending his lunch hour in the executive dining room. Company gossip reported that Hamilton had a thing for Krysta, and Krysta seemed to welcome the attention. Jack would have loved to find something to criticize about Hamilton, but there wasn't much

wrong with him except a slight tendency toward ner-
diness. In today's world, that might be a plus, he
thought.

"Excuse me for interrupting, but I have the symphony tickets for tomorrow night," Derek said. "Shall I
pick you up about sixish? We'll have a drink, and then
a light supper after the performance."

Krysta's answering smile made Jack clench his back
teeth together.

"That would be great, Derek," she said. "You know
Jack Killigan from shipping, don't you?"

Jack pushed back his chair and stood. Turning, he
stuck out his hand. Hamilton took it and initiated a
bone-crushing handshake, a technique Jack had en-
countered a few times from men shorter and slighter
than he was. After months of working on the dock, Jack
could have broken several bones in Hamilton's fingers
if he chose to retaliate.

He didn't. Hamilton had the power to get him fired,
and he still needed a regular paycheck to support his
writing habit. The job was perfect, a purely physical
one so he could keep his brain fresh for the nightly
writing sessions. "Nice to see you, Mr. Hamilton," he
said.

"For heaven's sake, call me Derek." Derek retrieved
his hand. "Shipping's one of our most efficient depart-
ments. I'm glad to meet one of its members."

"Jack's family and mine know each other back in
Mount Vernon," Krysta said.

Jack wished she hadn't felt obligated to explain that,
as if that was the only reason she was sitting at the table with him. Maybe it was. What a depressing
thought.

"Really?" Derek looked relieved by the news that Jack was an old family friend. "It's a small world, isn't it?" With that, he made a show of consulting something that looked like a Rolex.

Jack observed the gesture with malicious intent. A Rolex second hand made a clean sweep of the dial; an imitation jerked with each second that passed. Hamilton's watch jerked. Jack smiled to himself.

"Gotta run," Hamilton said with breezy efficiency. "Big meeting with marketing in five minutes."

"Are you planning to present my idea?" Krysta asked.

"I certainly am. I'll tell you all about it tomorrow night."

Krysta's smile was dazzling as she looked at Hamilton. "See you then, Derek."

"What idea?" Jack asked when Hamilton was out of earshot. He didn't even want to think about the impending date for the symphony.

"Rainier's been researching materials other than lumber to use for making paper. I suggested doing an infomercial that might boost the company's image."

Jack nodded, impressed. "So Hamilton's going to present your idea to marketing?"

"That's right. And that's how you can get ahead, Jack," she continued. "By demonstrating your abilities to the people who count."

"Hamilton can count, too? The man's a veritable genius."

Krysta frowned. "That's so typical of you, joking around when I'm trying to make an important point."

He wasn't joking around. He really disliked the idea of her dating Hamilton, which wasn't fair. Hamilton had several things to offer Krysta that Jack couldn't, and he should be happy for her. "I'm sorry. Please make your important point. I'll be good."

"Just like they said in my management course last semester, it's important to make a plan and then follow it. And it's obvious to me you have no plan, Jack. If you had one you would have had more to say when meeting Derek, some discerning comment that would make him notice you."

"I thought about saying 'Love your fake Rolex.' Guess I should have."

She put her hand over her mouth but her eyes gave away the smile. She cleared her throat and composed her features. "You promised to be serious. And besides, that is *not* a fake. Derek told me he bought it from a reputable jeweler in Seattle."

"Probably the reputable kind who conducts business on the sidewalk."

"Your attitude is terrible. You know that, don't you?"

Jack grinned at her as he stretched his tired muscles. "Blame it on lack of sleep." He pushed back his chair and picked up his tray. "Well, gotta run. I have a meeting with a two-hundred-pound bale of paper in five minutes."

"Jack, Jack, Jack. I'm concerned about your future."

"That's okay. You have enough future for both of us." He stood. Then he paused and gave her a long look. "Remember, if you ever need anything, I'm here. And I'm a good listener."

The vulnerable expression returned. "Thanks, Jack."

He set down his tray and returned to his seat. So he'd be late. "Talk to me, Krysta."

Immediately her expression cleared, and she gave him a big smile as she stood. "Don't be silly. Everything's fine. But it won't be if we don't get our fannies back to work. See you tomorrow. And take the vitamin C."

THE FIRST WEEK IN JANUARY, Krysta came into the office earlier than usual to get a head-start on a contract that had to be finished that morning. Lately she felt like a person running a foot race on a frozen lake. The transfer to marketing didn't look as if it would happen anytime soon, and her personal relationship with Derek was becoming sticky. He was pressuring her to go to bed with him, and she'd discovered that no matter how hard she tried to be attracted to him, he left her cold.

On paper Derek was everything she wanted in a man. He had position, reasonably good looks, ambition and cultured tastes. And he was polite and considerate. But he was also as boring as broccoli and his kisses made her gag. She'd never have guessed that would happen, and it was extremely inconvenient. Instead of making an ally of Derek she chanced making him an enemy if she kept holding him off.

Then last week her nineteen-year-old brother Henry had lost his part-time job, which meant he'd need a subsidy in order to continue in college until he could find another job. And her brother Joe had been offered a scholarship at the University of Puget Sound in Tacoma, which was where he wanted to go, but it clinched the need for live-in help for her father beginning in September.

And to top everything off, Jack Killigan hadn't improved one whit. He'd dawdled about enrolling in a night class and missed the cutoff date. He still hadn't gotten a decent haircut, and his dark hair was longer and more unruly than ever. Down in shipping they'd started making him tie it back in a ponytail while he worked. He still held the earpiece of his glasses together with tape, ate an atrocious diet and seemed to get no sleep whatsoever. She'd considered giving up on him and telling her father and the Killigans that it was no use trying to save Jack from himself. But every once in a while the fatigue would fall away from Jack's blue eyes and they'd shine with an intelligence that took her breath away. So she soldiered on, although she appeared to be wasting valuable time on him.

With a sigh Krysta turned on her computer and called up the file with the contract that needed to be finished.

A few minutes later, Rosie came in and hung up her trench coat. "No word on the marketing department job yet, huh?"

"No." Krysta looked up from the screen. "I'm surprised, considering they're using the infomercial idea I suggested through Derek. That should have made an impression on somebody." She reached for her coffee mug, but paused in midmotion. Jack Killigan had just walked through the door. To her knowledge he'd never set foot in her office in the eight months he'd worked for Rainier Paper.

Rosie turned toward the door, obviously motivated by the expression on Krysta's face. Rosie glanced at the name embroidered over the chest pocket of Jack's coveralls and smiled. "You're Jack." She held out her hand. "We've never met because I'm one of those people who blow their money going out for lunch, but Krysta's mentioned you."

Jack shook her hand and returned the smile, but he seemed very distracted. "She probably told you I'm a hopeless case."

"She did, as a matter of fact."

By this time, the agitation evident in Jack's manner had Krysta on her feet and moving toward him. "What is it? Has something happened?"

"I wondered if I could talk to you for a minute."

"Sure."

He glanced at Rosie. "Uh, in private?"

Krysta frowned. She'd never seen him like this, so full of nervous energy that he couldn't stand in one place. "There's a little conference room down the hall. We can go there."

"Great."

She led the way out the door, and he fell into step beside her as they moved down the carpeted hallway. They met Juliet Bancroft coming toward them, hurrying as she glanced at her watch. She gave Krysta a puzzled look.

Krysta paused. "I'll be back in a minute. I know you want to go over the Stevenson Corporation agreement first thing. I'm already working on it."

"That's good," Juliet said. "Derek said he wanted it ready by ten."

"It will be." Krysta had noticed Derek was setting tighter deadlines for the contracts department lately. She figured he was getting pressure from above to improve efficiency.

As she and Jack continued down the hall, she expected some crack about Derek, but Jack stayed uncharacteristically silent. She became more curious than ever as to why he was so preoccupied.

She opened the door to the windowless conference room and flipped on the overhead lights. A polished wooden table and eight chairs upholstered in blue tweed commandeered most of the space, and a large dry-erase message board covered with diagrams from a recent meeting dominated the wall at the end of the table.

Jack closed the door behind them and glanced around.

Krysta pulled out a chair that rolled easily on its casters and sat down. "Is this private enough?"

"I guess so." Jack moved around her to the next chair, but he leaned against the back instead of sitting in it. He pushed his glasses up on his nose and glanced at her. "I don't know quite how to explain this."

"You're in trouble with the law and they've tracked you down?" She'd always wondered what he'd been up to after he quit college and went adventuring around the countryside for several years.

The corner of his mouth lifted. "You don't think very highly of my character, do you?"

"Jack, people can usually put past mistakes behind them. Maybe I can vouch for you when—"

"Okay, I'll just say it." He gripped the back of the chair. "I've been spending all my nights writing books."

Whatever she'd been expecting, it wasn't this. She stared at him.

"So far I've only had rejections." He pushed away from the chair and took a deep breath. "Then yesterday Manchester Publishing called my apartment, and they want me to call back today, collect, and..." He paused. "God, I'm so afraid to jinx this by saying it out loud."

"You've sold a book?" She couldn't have been more shocked if he'd revealed that he was an international jewel thief.

"I think so." Suddenly his grin flashed full wattage. "Yeah, Krysta. Yeah, I think I finally did it."

"Jack, that's marvelous!" She sent the chair thumping against its neighbor as she leaped to her feet and threw her arms around his neck. "I knew you weren't a loser!" And then, surprising them both, she kissed him soundly on the mouth.

KRYSTA HAD A BRIEF few seconds to register a citrus-scented after-shave, a mouth that fit almost perfectly against hers, a solid chest, and a very pleasant zing of feeling before she came to her senses and pulled away. Kissing Jack! She must be out of her mind. In all the years the Killigans and the Lueckenhoffs had been friends, she'd never thought of Jack in that way. Never.

She put a hand to her heart and steadied her breathing. Somehow she had to pretend she hadn't just done such a ridiculous thing. Jack was like one of her brothers, for heaven's sake.

"So all this time," she began, her voice quivering only a little, "when I thought you were a couch potato, you've been writing a book?" she said.

He gazed at her without speaking for several seconds. Finally he cleared his throat and pushed back the glasses she'd dislodged. "Several books, actually. That's why I've been working on the dock. It's the perfect job for a writer, because I don't have to think much and I still feel creative when I get to my computer each night."

She shook her head, dazed by his revelation. No wonder she'd reacted so uncharacteristically and kissed him. "We need to tell your parents, Jack. They should know that you—"

"Absolutely not."

"But Jack, they think you're a lost cause!"

"First of all, we don't know yet if I've sold this book because I haven't called Manchester Publishing, and second of all, I'm not sure my parents will be all that impressed when they do find out."

She was slowly regaining her poise, although her lips still tingled. "Of course they will. And why haven't you called the publisher back? It's—" she glanced at her watch. "—already ten minutes after eleven in New York! Another half hour and they might be at lunch! What are you waiting for?"

"You."

She really shouldn't have kissed him. No telling what sort of ideas he might get from that. The kiss meant nothing, of course, but in her experience men tended to respond quickly to such stimulation. She schooled her expression into a professional mask. "I don't understand."

"I wrote a romance."

"A what?"

"You know. A love story. Manchester was having a Valentine's Day contest for unpublished writers and I—"

"I *know* what a romance is, Jack. I read them all the time. I just can't picture you writing one."

"Why?"

She opened her mouth to reply.

"Never mind." He sounded vaguely irritated. "I'm not sure I want to hear your answer. At any rate, I was afraid the publishers would react exactly the way you're reacting if I sent the book in under my own name, so I made up a woman's name, figuring that would help my cause. I don't know if it did or not, but

I'm not taking any chances on messing things up now. I want you to call and pretend you wrote the book."

"Me?" She drew in a lungful of air. "I don't think so."

"Please, Krysta. You're the only one I can trust to do this."

"No, Jack! They could ask me something about the book, and I won't know what it's about or anything. Just tell them who you are."

"I promise there'll be nothing to it. If they want to buy, they'll probably offer me—you—a contract. All you have to do is accept it. If they start talking about the book, just say you'd rather have those comments in a letter because you're better at visual communication."

Krysta's eyes narrowed. "Did I just hear you say that all I have to do is accept the contract?"

"That's right. Just accept it and get off the phone."

"Oh, no, you don't!"

He looked puzzled. "Oh, no I don't what?"

"You *never* just accept a contract. You *always* negotiate."

"You don't understand. I would pay *them* to publish this if I had the money. I don't care what they offer, as long as the book will come out. It's a reputable publisher. I don't think they'll try to low-ball me. But even if they did, I wouldn't care."

Krysta was beginning to understand the situation and now realized she needed to make this phone call for Jack. As usual, he wasn't prepared to watch out for his own interests. "Okay, I'll do it."

His eyes sparkled. "You will? Fantastic!"

"When did you want me to make the call?"

"I thought we could call from your office during the lunch hour, when everybody's gone. I don't want anybody else to know about this yet."

"Why not? You'll be a published author, for heaven's sake. Not many people can say that." Her mental image of Jack was undergoing a rapid transformation. And she'd thought he had no enterprise in his soul. She'd been so wrong.

"Well, for one thing, the guys down on the shipping dock will never give me a moment's peace if they find out I wrote a book. Then, if they find out it's a romance, my life won't be worth living."

She nodded. "I see your point. Romance writing is rather an unusual field for men." She had a million questions about how a smart-mouthed guy like Jack had managed to write such a book, but she had to get back to the Stevenson contract before she put her own job in jeopardy. "Well, you can trust me to keep your secret."

"I know that."

She looked past the disreputable glasses into blue eyes that for a moment held hers captive. Her stomach gave a funny little lurch, and she glanced away. She couldn't imagine what was wrong with her. She'd looked into Jack's eyes a thousand times before, and her stomach had always behaved itself. "Why don't you come up to the office about fifteen minutes after twelve?" she said. "Everyone else will be gone, and you can listen in on the conversation when I make the call."

"Perfect." He reached for her wrist and looked at her watch. "We're both late. I'll probably catch hell. See you then." He was out the door and loping down the hall before she could say anything.

She stood in the open doorway and looked after him while she unconsciously massaged her wrist. When she realized what she was doing she stopped and glanced down at the spot where his fingers had gripped her gently. Her skin seemed to vibrate where he'd touched her. In all the years of playing tag, arm wrestling and exchanging high-fives, she never remembered a tingle like that. It was disconcerting, to say the least.

JACK BARELY AVOIDED maiming himself while working on the shipping dock that morning. A potential book sale and a kiss from Krysta in the same day would be distracting enough on a full night's sleep, let alone on the two hours' rest he'd allowed himself between four and six.

He wandered in front of moving forklifts without looking and came within a half inch of dropping a paper bale on his foot. Fortunately the guys in shipping were used to his muddled ways, and for some reason the foreman had taken a liking to him and routinely excused his blunders. If he had to hold down a regular job, he couldn't ask for a better one than this. And there was also the fringe benefit of seeing Krysta every day.

As kids growing up together they'd never dated, partly because they'd known each other too well and there was none of the mystery so critical for teenage romance, and partly because Krysta had been too much of a goody-two-shoes for Jack's tastes at the time. Then they hadn't seen each other for years, until he landed this job at Rainier. Her attitude toward him had remained exactly the same, but Jack had taken one look at Krysta and wondered how he could have been such an idiot for all those years.

Unfortunately, Hamilton had already gained the inside track when Jack arrived on the scene. Besides, Krysta had never given Jack the slightest indication she regarded him as anything other than an old friend. Until this morning. Not that he should put much importance on that kiss. She'd reacted on impulse and caught herself right away. But for a moment...

Finally noon arrived and he clocked out for lunch, washed up and headed for the service elevator. His stomach grumbled from nervousness and lack of food. He wondered if he could be building castles in the air. The night before he'd played the phone message over and over until he had it memorized.

This is Stephanie Briggs, senior editor at Manchester Publishing, calling for Candace Johnson about your manuscript Uptown Girl. *I'd like to discuss the book with you. Please call me collect at your earliest convenience.*

Then she'd given the number and her extension. He couldn't believe an editor would give that out unless she was serious about a manuscript. But then again, he still had a lot to learn about this business. He had to prepare himself for anything. By the time he walked into the contracts office, he was sweating.

"You look awful," Krysta observed helpfully.

"Thanks. I feel as if a whole bowling team is practicing in my gut." But he felt calmer from the moment he saw her sitting there, perfectly groomed in her kelly green suit and white silky blouse, her hair burnished as if she'd just given it a hundred strokes with a hairbrush. A chair was positioned beside her desk. He took it and drew a deep breath. "Got a pencil? I'll give you the number."

She lifted her eyebrows. "You didn't write it down?"

"Didn't have to." He was loathe to admit he'd played the message about a hundred times and wouldn't be able to forget the phone number if someone gave him a lobotomy.

He recited the number, and although she shook her head in disapproval, she wrote it carefully on a notepad. She put a line across her sevens, European style, and he found that kind of sexy.

"You're calling Stephanie Briggs, senior editor at Manchester Publishing," he added, and Krysta wrote that down, too, her writing full of little angles and squiggles that intrigued him. He realized he could be quite happy sitting here for hours watching her do her job. "And your name is Candace Johnson."

Her gaze flicked up from the notepad and met his. "Candace, like your mother?"

"Yes. Candace and John's son," he finished for her. "I know it's corny, and they might not appreciate it when it appears on a book jacket, but I needed a woman's name, so I came up with that."

"I think you're wrong about your parents. I think they'll be very impressed."

He grinned at her. "That their only son is masquerading as a woman?"

"Oh, for heaven's sake. I think it's a wonderful choice, and so will they."

"Besides, *J* is close to the middle of the alphabet, so on a bookstore shelf the book will show up about eye level."

She gave him an approving glance. "It's good to

know you can think in practical terms sometimes." She wrote the pseudonym on the notepad. "Candace Johnson. I think it's perfect." She looked up at him again. "What's the name of your book?"

Gazing into the warmth of her eyes, he couldn't remember.

"Jack?"

"Uh, *Uptown Girl.*"

She glanced down at the notepad and started to write. Then she paused. "I can't remember if *uptown* has a hyphen."

"No hyphen." Released from the magic pull of her gaze, he was able to regain his equilibrium and smile at her perfectionistic tendencies. "But I don't think that will matter on the phone."

"You're right. I'm just so used to typing faxes." She finished writing and tore the paper from the pad with a crisp movement. "I really wish I knew more about this book, Jack."

"All right. Here's a quick synopsis. Jake, a guy from the wrong side of the tracks, falls in love with a CEO's daughter, Christine, after they accidentally spend the night together. She doesn't want anything more than a fling and they part. Jake becomes a labor leader fighting her dad's company. A bunch of stuff happens, but in the climactic scene, she chooses Jake and his world over life in the fast lane." He watched her expression to see if a heroine named Christine would alert her to his use of her as inspiration but no awareness dawned.

"Sounds good." She regarded him with interest. "I guess I didn't know you as well as I thought when we were growing up. You never seemed to take anything very seriously. I had no idea you wanted to write."

"Neither did I. The only reason I went to college was because they offered me a football scholarship. Then I took a writing class because somebody said it was an easy credit. That class hit me like a lightning bolt, and I suddenly knew how I wanted to spend the rest of my life."

"Then why on earth did you drop out of college? I would think more classes—"

"Nope." Jack shook his head. "My writing teacher was very unusual. She said I had a gift for storytelling, and too much time in creative writing classes might screw that up. She suggested I spend a few years gathering experiences and reading all kinds of popular fiction instead of sitting in classrooms. I think she was right."

Krysta frowned. "I'm not sure I agree with that advice, but I can't argue with the results."

"We don't know what the results are yet," he reminded her, his anxiety returning.

"Oh, yes we do. They want this book, Jack." She pushed back her chair. "You sit here at my desk and I'll use Rosie's so we can see each other and give hand signals." She pointed to a desk directly across the room that faced hers. Then she pushed a button on her telephone. "I'll use that line. When I give you the thumbs-up sign, you pick up the receiver, very, very carefully."

His hands had begun to shake. "Maybe I shouldn't try to listen in."

"Nonsense. I want you to hear all the wonderful things that—" she consulted the paper in her hand. "—Stephanie Briggs has to say about your writing."

He sat at her desk while she crossed to Rosie's and

settled herself there. Then she grinned at him and started to dial.

He gripped the arms of her chair as if he were in a rocket about to launch. Eager for distractions, he skimmed a glance across her desk and noted the monogrammed desk accessories, a bud vase with a single pink rose—probably from Hamilton—and a framed photograph taken at the beach of her brothers and her father. Jack remembered vividly the winter sixteen years ago when her mother had died. It had been his first funeral. At the ripe-old age of eleven, Krysta had taken charge of the family of four younger brothers and a handicapped father. No wonder she was such a dedicated little caretaker.

Then he heard Krysta give her information for the collect call to the long distance operator, and he looked across the office, his stomach churning. She raised her fist, thumb pointed at the ceiling.

Although he doubted he'd be able to hear anything over the roaring in his ears, he reached a shaky hand toward the receiver.

"Ms. Briggs?" Krysta said, sounding cool and professional. "I'm Candace Johnson."

Jack fumbled the receiver and cursed under his breath.

Krysta winced at the noise. "Sorry about that, Ms. Briggs. These darn shoulder gadgets for the phone are a nuisance, aren't they?"

Jack brought the receiver to his ear in time to hear Stephanie Briggs laugh.

"I take it you're calling from an office, then," said the senior editor.

"Yes. I work for Rainier Paper here in Evergreen."

Jack frowned. He wouldn't have volunteered that. Too much information might be dangerous.

"Really?" Stephanie said. "So you're one of those stalwarts who works a day job and writes by night."

"That's right," Krysta said, glancing across at Jack. "Existing mostly on sugar and caffeine."

Jack made a face at her and she winked back.

"I'm always impressed with the things writers sacrifice for their craft," Stephanie said. "But now comes the reward for all that lost sleep, Candace. *Uptown Girl* is wonderful. You're the hands-down winner of our Valentine's Day new author contest, and I'd like to make you an offer on your book."

Jack nearly dropped the receiver, and even Krysta lost her cool for a second as she yelped into the phone and punched her fist in the air.

Stephanie's tone was indulgent. "I rather thought you'd be pleased."

Krysta took a more professional tone. "Yes, I am. And I'm delighted that you like *Uptown Girl*. It's special to me, too."

Jack drew his finger quickly across his throat to signal Krysta to shut up. She was getting carried away with the moment and heading straight for trouble.

"I can tell that it is," Stephanie said. "That scene when they both fall in the drainage ditch and later wash each other clean is incredibly sensuous. I wondered what your inspiration was for that."

Krysta's eyes snapped open wide and she looked straight at Jack. "Uh, well, you know we have a lot of water here in western Washington, Ms. Briggs."

Stephanie laughed. "Call me Stephanie. And of course you're right. That explains all the water images.

The rain scene, and the time they make love beside the waterfall in the park. You have a deft touch with love scenes, which is critical to our readership."

"Th-thank you." Krysta focused on Jack, her gaze curious.

He kept his expression purposely blank.

"I also wondered if Candace Johnson is your real name or a pseudonym?"

Jack sat up straighter.

"It's a pseudonym," Krysta said smoothly. "But I plan to use it as my professional name, so you may certainly call me Candace."

Jack relaxed a little.

"Then if it's not your legal name at this point, would you consider changing it slightly?" Stephanie asked.

Krysta lifted her eyebrows as she gazed at Jack.

To what? he mouthed to her.

"To what?" Krysta repeated to Stephanie.

"Well, your first name actually started us down this road. Our vice president in charge of marketing suggested Candy instead of Candace."

Jack winced. He'd pretty much accepted the idea of using a feminine name, but Candy was a little further than he'd planned to go.

"I personally prefer Candace," Krysta said.

But then again, Jack decided, he'd be Minnie Mouse if it would help the sale of the book. He got Krysta's attention and was about to signal her to accept the nickname when Stephanie spoke again.

"Well, it would be up to you, of course, but marketing has a whole campaign mapped out, and it's going to be dynamite. By this time next year Candy Valentine's novel will be the talk of the publishing world."

Jack stared at Krysta, who stared right back, obviously in shock.

"Excuse me?" she said at last.

"Candy Valentine. We hadn't thought of it until we looked at Candace and started tossing ideas around. Sure, it's hokey, but that's okay. In fact, it's more than okay for this Valentine's Day promotion we have lined up. And believe me, with Valentine as a pseudonym, you'll own the holiday, hands down."

"But—but won't the book be on the bottom of the racks, shelved under *V*?" Krysta asked.

Stephanie laughed. "No, dear. You'll have your own thirty-six-pocket display dump in the front of the store."

Krysta looked frantically across at Jack for some direction. Bless her, he thought. Despite the lure of a thirty-six-pocket display dump, she didn't want to sacrifice his precious pseudonym without his permission. He closed his eyes, silently apologized to his parents and nodded his assent. Candy Valentine. Good Lord.

"Well, in that case, I guess Candy Valentine it is." Krysta made a face at Jack.

"Good. That kind of team spirit will come in handy during the next year. And speaking of that, let's get to the nuts and bolts of this offer. We'll pay you half the advance upon signing the contract, and the second half when the book is accepted for publication."

"Isn't it already accepted?" Krysta asked.

"Essentially, but I have some revision suggestions, and I'm turning the book over to an assistant editor, so I'm sure she'll have some suggestions, too. Once you've completed the revisions and they've been accepted, the second half of the advance will be paid."

"But you're planning this big campaign, even though the deal isn't really final?"

"Oh, we have to, in the interests of time. If, in the end, the book isn't acceptable, we'll just have to change our plans. I doubt that would happen, but this is how the publishing world works, Candy."

"I see."

Jack watched Krysta's expression become intent. She'd obviously slipped into her business mode.

"And what is the advance?" she asked without a quiver of uncertainty in her voice.

Stephanie named an amount that Jack thought sounded quite fair considering it was his first book.

Krysta tapped her pen against the blotter and let a full three seconds elapse before she answered. "That's quite low, wouldn't you say, Stephanie?"

Once again Jack had to make a grab for the receiver, which he almost dropped. He pushed back his chair and stood, waving an arm frantically at Krysta.

"Low?" Stephanie seemed at a loss for words. "It's our standard advance for a first book."

"That may be true, but you said *Uptown Girl* is wonderful. And you're planning to put it in a thirty-six-pocket display dump. Surely you expect to make a lot of money."

Jack moved around to the front of the desk and as far as the telephone cord would reach in an effort to get to Krysta before she ruined his life. The cord was a good six feet too short.

"The book is wonderful, and we *hope* to make money," Stephanie said. "But—"

"Would you say it's better than your standard first book?" Krysta asked.

Jack danced, waved and cursed silently. Krysta gazed at him for a moment before swiveling her desk chair around to face the wall.

"Yes, I suppose it is better than the usual," Stephanie said.

"Twice as good?"

Jack closed his eyes. He was doomed.

"Perhaps," Stephanie said cautiously. "But I warn you that overpaying on a first book can backfire. If you don't earn out the advance, then—"

"It will earn out," Krysta cut in. "And I want twice your original offer."

Jack stifled a groan of despair. The chance of a lifetime, and it was slipping through his fingers because he'd allowed Donald Trump to negotiate the deal.

"I'll have to discuss this with a few people," Stephanie said.

"That's fine."

No, that's not fine, Jack raged to himself. *It's over.*

"I'll call you back in a couple of hours."

"Good. I'll still be at the office then. You can contact me here." Krysta gave the number of Rainier Paper and her extension. "It was nice talking to you, Stephanie."

"Same here, Candy. We'll be in touch." There was a solid click.

Jack practically threw the receiver into its cradle. "Are you insane? You killed my sale!"

Krysta swiveled around to face him, replaced her receiver with care and steepled her fingers. "You were ready to give that book away for nothing, weren't you?"

"Yes!" Jack shoved his glasses back on his nose with

a vengeance. "Because it would have been a beginning! A huge beginning! My own display in the front of the store! The money doesn't matter."

"The money always matters. If you don't value what you do, others won't value it either."

"This is *not* the time to take a stand on money." He pointed a finger at her. "I can guarantee you they won't call back. They'll choose another winner for the contest, and next week the manuscript will arrive in the mail, just like all the rest, and—"

"No, it won't. Weren't you listening to her? They like the book, Jack."

"Not twice as much, they don't." He paced in front of Rosie's desk. "I can't believe you did this. I wonder if you could call back and say that you'd had a little out-of-body experience just now, and you'd be willing to accept the original offer."

"I'd refuse to do that, even if you were dumb enough to ask me! You're lucky you had me call. If you'd done it, they'd immediately figure out they had a pushover on their hands and they'd probably take advantage of you."

He spun to face her. "And I wouldn't *care.* I want my name—or Candy's name—on a book jacket, Krysta. I've wanted to publish a novel for years. If Manchester will do that, they can push me over as many times as they'd like."

"Which is precisely why you need someone to take care of business for you." She folded her arms. "You're going to thank me for this, Jack. Now, shall we put all this aside for the time being and go down to the cafeteria and grab a quick bite?"

He stared at her. "How can you even think about eating at a time like this?"

"Relax." She stood and came around the desk. "They'll call back and you'll have more money. Trust me, this is the way to handle contract negotiations. Don't forget, I've spent two years in the contracts department here at Rainier, and I know this end of the business inside and out. You operate from strength, not weakness, independence, not neediness."

He had forgotten, in the excitement of having her agree to call for him. Belatedly he remembered that she'd made a point of saying a contract was never accepted without negotiation. He'd glossed right over that little statement of hers.

If he'd been paying better attention, he might not have asked her to make the call, although God knows who else he could have asked. Since taking this job and focusing on his writing, he'd given up all claim of having a social life. No, Krysta had been the only one he could turn to, and she'd shafted him. Unless by some miracle she was right. But he didn't think so.

"Come on." She took him by the arm and guided him toward the door. "You can even have cake and coffee today and I won't say a word."

3

HARD HATS WERE REQUIRED on the shipping dock, so when Jack saw Krysta approach him without one, his stomach churned. She was looking straight at him and not paying the slightest attention to what was going on around her. He hurried forward and guided her out through the double doors into the main part of the building. Once inside the tiled hall, he took off his hard hat and his safety goggles.

She turned to him. "Jack, I came to tell you—"

"I know what you came to tell me," he said in a voice tight with strain. He didn't want to hear this, but he especially didn't want to hear it in the hallway, where one of his fellow workers was heading toward them after a trip to the break room for a cigarette. "The foreman's office should be empty right now, since he's on the dock. We'll go in there." He indicated a gray metal door stenciled with Bud's name and position. "I don't think he locks it."

Fortunately Bud had left the office open, and they slipped inside the small enclosure that was barely big enough for the metal desk and the couple of chairs that occupied it.

Jack closed the door and put his goggles in his hard hat before tossing them on a chair. Then he faced her and steeled himself for the bad news. "Okay, what'd they say?"

She looked like a kid on Christmas morning. "They went for it."

"You're kidding." His brain refused to assimilate what she was saying. He'd decided during their brief lunch that he was incapable of staying angry with Krysta over this. It was his game, and he'd gambled and lost. The best thing to do was forget it and go on.

"No, I'm not kidding." She was so excited she was trembling. "Now, listen carefully, because maybe you'll learn a valuable lesson from this. Stephanie said she was impressed with my bargaining skills, and that she liked working with someone who valued her own talent."

Jack adjusted his glasses, as if that might make him hear better. "You're sure you understood her right?"

"They're buying it, Jack." Her voice hummed with delight. "For twice the amount."

The truth finally hit him, and without thinking, he grabbed her and swung her around, nearly colliding with the desk in the process. "They went for it! I sold a book! I really sold a book!"

"You sold a book!" she echoed, hugging him tight.

He glanced down at her. Her mouth was so close and he was so damned happy that he couldn't stop himself. A moment like this came once in a lifetime, and it deserved to be celebrated. As his lips touched hers, he knew this kiss would beat a bottle of Dom Pérignon any day.

He claimed her with all the triumph he felt, and she responded. Good Lord, did she respond. Within seconds he forgot about the book sale, the shipping dock and even Rainier Paper. There was only Krysta, coming alive in his arms, making him ache with a ferocity he hadn't allowed himself to feel in a long time.

Then, just as quickly, the moment ended as she eased away from him. Her face was pink and she lowered her gaze. "Congratulations."

He took a moment to get his bearings. Wow. "Thanks."

"Stephanie said she and the assistant editor would get their notes together on the revisions and send you a letter," she said, still not looking at him. "But you're not to touch the love scenes."

"Oh?" His heartbeat slowly returned to normal. "Why not?"

Krysta lifted her head and tried for an impersonal gaze. She almost succeeded. "The love scenes are luscious, I believe she said."

"Mm." His arms and chest still felt the imprint of her body, and her scent filled his nostrils. He'd better usher her out of here before he really overstepped his limits. He had to remember that she'd pushed him away. Nothing had really changed between them. "Well, I can't thank you enough. I guess we'd both better get back to work."

"I guess so. But there is one other thing, and I'm not sure what you want to do about it."

One other thing. He should have known. "They've decided not to publish the book for another three years?"

"No, no. Nothing like that. They want to stay on schedule with the Valentine's Day promotion next year, just like Stephanie said on the phone. But before I hung up, she asked for a bio."

His anxiety level dropped several notches. "No

problem. I'll just leave out the football and emphasize the writing class. A bio doesn't have to reveal my gender."

"That's true, but I think a picture will."

"They want a picture of me?"

"No, they want a picture of Candy Valentine."

He cringed anew at the pseudonym. "I hope you told them you weren't photogenic. Ugly, even."

"I tried, but she said they didn't care. I said I had nothing recent, but that didn't matter to her, either. She was getting very suspicious, and I was afraid she might start asking the wrong questions, so finally I agreed to come up with something."

Jack rubbed the back of his neck. Then he glanced at her. "Would you consider it?"

"Sending a picture of me? I don't know what else we can do."

He caught her use of "we." She considered herself part of this project now. At least there was that. "I'd sure appreciate it if you could find a picture, then. This should be the last thing I have to ask of you."

"It's no problem, really. I believe in finishing what I start. And obviously this isn't quite finished."

"No," Jack said, gazing at her and remembering the explosive nature of their kiss. "I guess not."

AT LUNCH THE NEXT DAY Krysta sat down and placed a manila envelope next to her tray. "I went home last night and started going through pictures, but I didn't have very many of myself." She glanced at Jack. Much as she tried to retain the sisterly attitude she'd always had toward him, it was slipping fast. "I guess people don't keep a lot of pictures of themselves around. Just of other people." She didn't mention that while searching for the right picture she'd replayed their shared kisses many times over in her mind. That second kiss had really rocked her. She'd never been kissed with such abandon or responded with such gusto herself. Thank God she'd come to her senses and pulled away. Once again she'd put her reaction down to the unusual nature of the moment. Discovering Jack wasn't the person she'd imagined had flustered her more than a little.

"I hope you didn't spend much time on this picture business." He slathered his hot dog with mustard. "We're just throwing something at them to satisfy their public relations department."

"You sound as if appearances don't matter."

"They don't, in this case. All that really matters is the manuscript." He took a large bite.

As she watched him ingest the preservative-filled hot dog she reminded herself that although he might have given her the most exciting kiss of her life, he was still just plain Jack, a guy who needed direction, both in matters of diet and business. She'd concentrate on the most important first. "I agree the manuscript is important, but so is your image. Stephanie already has a mental picture of Candy Valentine as a competent, imaginative person with a lot of confidence in herself. The picture we send should support that mental image."

He finished chewing and swallowed. "How can we miss? You're a competent, imaginative person with a lot of confidence in yourself. I'm sure that comes across on camera." He reached for the envelope. "Let's see what you've got."

"Wait." She snatched it back. "Let me present them

and explain my reasoning for each one. Then we'll choose."

He chuckled and shook his head. "Good thing I didn't let you proofread my manuscript. It'd probably still be in rewrites while you searched for that last little typo."

She gasped. "You didn't send it in with *mistakes*, did you, Jack?"

He leaned toward her, his blue eyes serious behind the wire-rimmed glasses. "Yes, Krysta, I probably did, exhausted as I was. But I threw caution to the winds and sent it in, anyway. And look what happened."

"You were lucky!" She wondered how Jack had made it this far in life, disorganized and sloppy as he seemed to be. "Mistakes undermine your credibility. I'm certainly glad I didn't know about this before I bargained on your behalf yesterday. I might not have had the confidence to push so hard, knowing there were probably misplaced commas and heaven knows what else lurking in that manuscript."

"Lots of good sex."

She looked into his eyes and saw the teasing light there, but behind the teasing burned a more potent fire, one that brought back the memory of their explosive kiss from the day before. "So Stephanie said." She took a quick gulp of water and opened the envelope. "Okay. I narrowed it down to three."

"Sounds like plenty of choices to me."

"I'm not so sure." She pulled out the top one, a black and white shot she'd had taken to mail out with her resume three years ago. "This is actually the most correct thing to send. But it may be too polished for someone who's just a beginner. Not spontaneous enough, after the way I protested about sending a picture in the first place."

Jack took the picture by the edges. She was surprised he handled it with such care, given his general tendencies.

He studied it intently before looking up at her with a critical eye. "The photographer didn't capture your spirit. This is quite beautiful, but it's also a little flat."

She bristled. "He's an excellent photographer with a studio in Seattle. I told him I wanted this for professional purposes, and I think he made me look very professional. Derek complimented me on that picture when he saw it in the personnel files."

"I'm sure he did. It's Hamilton's sort of picture."

"Which points out his good business sense. This picture helped me get the job here at Rainier. You're awfully hard on Derek, Jack. He's never done anything to you, and you could probably learn some things from him that would help you now that you're moving into a new career."

He looked so much like a belligerent little boy who'd been chastised that she laughed. "Be honest, now. Derek is not a bad guy."

The belligerence cleared from his eyes and he smiled. "You're right. In fact, he's a real inspiration."

She didn't trust that kind of turnaround from a man like Jack. And she had a new respect for his use of words now that she knew about his writing. "That didn't sound particularly sincere."

"It should, because I mean it." He shifted in his chair. "What else do you have?"

She picked up the second photograph, one of her sitting in Juliet Bancroft's gazebo during a garden party

Juliet had hosted for Rainier employees the previous summer. Krysta had borrowed a lace dress and picture hat from Rosie's sister for the event, which had been held a couple of weeks before Jack had begun work at the paper plant. Juliet had taken the picture, saying Krysta looked like something out of *Victoria* magazine against the latticework of the gazebo and a riot of climbing pink roses. That party was where Derek had first noticed her.

"Now, this is certainly romantic enough to be Candy Valentine." She handed it to him, waiting while he wiped mustard from his hands with a napkin. "Maybe too romantic," she added. "They might not take a woman like this seriously enough. But I thought you might go for this one, so I put it in."

Jack's gaze softened as he looked at the picture. Once again he glanced up at her, as if to compare the real woman with the photograph. "Better. Much better. But deceptive. You're not this sweet."

"I beg your pardon!"

He laughed, which dislodged his glasses. He pushed them back up on his nose and grinned at her. "Sorry. But remember that I listened in on the extension while you put the screws to Stephanie Briggs, esteemed senior editor of the prestigious Manchester Publishing House. You won't be able to pull the demure routine on me any more."

She couldn't help smiling. He was absolutely right, and after the first shock of indignation she discovered she preferred his assessment of her to Derek's, who had recently thought he was complimenting her by telling her she was a "lovely, uncomplicated girl." Derek underestimated her, and maybe that was one reason why she couldn't warm to him.

"Hey, nice pictures," Bud, the foreman from shipping, commented as he walked past their table carrying a loaded tray. He paused to look at the studio portrait and the gazebo shot. Then he glanced at Krysta. "You entering some beauty contest or something?"

Her brain went blank.

"She has a pen pal in Tasmania, and she was wondering what picture to send to her," Jack said smoothly.

"Oh." Bud consulted the pictures again. "The roses one. The other one doesn't look very friendly."

"Thanks," Krysta said.

"Anytime. And next time you pay us a visit in shipping, get a hard hat from my office first, okay?"

"I promise."

Bud looked at Jack. "See you at the dock in twenty minutes, Killigan. You can't make us any money looking at pen pal pictures."

"Right."

As Bud moved out of earshot, Krysta let out a sigh of relief. "You came up with that pretty fast, Jack."

"Don't forget I write fiction. And we do have to hurry along. What's the last one you brought?"

She withdrew the final picture, a snapshot her brother Ned had taken of her during the Father's Day picnic on the beach. Everyone had brought cameras and they'd produced a stack of shots—the free-for-all volleyball game, everyone taking turns cooking hamburgers, the furious activity surrounding the sand castle they'd built, and her father hoisting a beer with a happy smile on his face. Then, at sunset, Ned had posed Krysta against the same gnarled piece of driftwood she'd used for her shot of her father and his sons. The breeze had ruffled her hair and the joy of the day shone from her face.

Jack took one look at the picture and nodded. "That's it."

"I don't know. I mean, shorts and a halter top aren't very professional. I'm even barefoot, and my hair's all askew."

"It's perfect." Jack focused on the picture. "Who took it?"

"Ned. Why?"

"He has a great eye. Maybe he should go into it professionally."

"I don't know. Isn't that kind of a risky occupation?"

He glanced at her. "Every occupation is risky. Today's hot career is tomorrow's unemployment line. You can't guarantee those four brothers of yours a steady living, Krysta."

She lifted her chin. "Maybe not, but I want them to have a darned good head start, which means getting a degree. You may do fine without one, but you're the exception."

He regarded her steadily. "I'd say your brothers' greatest asset is having you there cheering them on."

"Oh, I doubt that." Her cheeks warmed.

"I don't. At least Ned knows your value. He's captured it in this picture. Is it the only print?"

She became more embarrassed. "Well, no. All my brothers reacted like you have to the picture, and Ned had to make copies for everyone. My dad has an eight-by-ten on his dresser. I told Ned he certainly didn't have to make a print for me, but he said he might as well as long as he was getting copies. He told me to give it to a boyfriend or something."

"So how come Hamilton doesn't have it?"

It was a puzzling question she had no answer to. "I guess I forgot," she said.

"His loss, then." Jack opened the flap of the chest pocket on his coveralls and tucked the picture carefully inside.

She still had misgivings about such an informal shot. "Are you sure that's the right one? To be honest, all three of them have some drawback, in my opinion. I even considered getting somebody to take a roll of me so we'd have more choices."

Jack shook his head. "Somebody could take six rolls of film and not get anything better than this." He patted his pocket. "You look happy, confident, full of life. If they need a mental picture of Candy, this is the one I want them to have."

She realized she'd just lost control of the decision. She was used to Jack being more tentative, but in this matter he seemed to know exactly what he wanted, and he didn't plan to consult her further. Well, it was his career, after all, even if it was her picture he was using.

He glanced at the clock on the cafeteria wall and pushed himself away from the table. "I'd better get back to the dock. Thanks for the picture, Krysta. This really should be the last thing I have to bother you about."

"It's no bother. I've enjoyed it."

He smiled. "Especially the power negotiating part, right?"

"It worked, didn't it?"

"Yes, I have to admit it worked. Left to my own devices, I would have been a poorer man."

"When will you get the money?"

"Not for a while, I suppose. I've read some magazine articles that say it can be weeks or even months before the contract shows up. Then I have to sign it and return it before the first check will arrive."

"Don't you dare sign that contract without letting me go over it, Jack Killigan."

He winked at her. "Pretty soon I'll have to offer you a cut for all this business management advice."

"You most certainly will not! I'm helping you out of friendship, Jack."

He picked up his tray and gazed at her. "And you've been a good friend, Krysta," he said. Then he turned and walked toward the tray cart.

Krysta watched him leave the cafeteria, his physique disguised by the bulky coveralls that everyone in shipping had to wear. She'd never paid much attention to his body before. After all, he'd been just plain Jack, the happy-go-lucky Killigan kid, a boy going nowhere. Not the sort of person Krysta, who planned to do something significant with her life, could relate to.

But she'd related to him with embarrassing enthusiasm when he'd kissed her yesterday. She'd become aware of broad shoulders, strong arms, and a very talented mouth, attributes she'd never associated with Jack Killigan before.

She needed to forget that kiss, because she had no intention of becoming involved with Jack. Perhaps she hadn't guessed that he was a writer but otherwise she knew his personality very well. He wasn't at all her type.

4

AFTER KRYSTA PROVIDED the snapshot of her at the beach, Jack's view over his computer improved considerably. Before he sent the picture to Manchester Publishing, he took it to a print shop and had them copy it as a two-by-three-foot poster that he tacked on the wall. His second romance novel had been going pretty well, but with the extra advantage of Krysta smiling at him with such tenderness every night, he found his fingers flying over the keys.

His villain was taking shape nicely, too, thanks to Krysta's suggestion that Derek Hamilton could be useful to him in his new career. Jack agreed with Krysta that Derek wasn't such a terrible guy, and he probably didn't deserve being skewered as the villain in this book, but Jack took great pleasure in doing it, anyway.

And Jack's stray cat had a name. One night as he was petting the cat's thick fur he realized it had much the same shading and color as Krysta's hair, which might have been why he'd allowed the cat to adopt him in the first place. Even the cat's green eyes reminded him of Krysta's.

He should have figured out sooner why he'd developed such an affinity for the animal, but he'd probably tried not to acknowledge his growing feelings for a woman he couldn't have. She had her sights firmly set on the likes of Derek, and if that was what she wanted, that was what he wanted her to get.

He'd counseled himself to be satisfied with the friendship they shared, which had been strengthened by their collaboration on his career. Every lunch hour she'd begin the conversation by asking if he'd seen any sign of the contract yet, because without that he couldn't begin to expect his first check.

Krysta had spent that money several times over. A haircut was first on the list, but that wouldn't take much. Then she'd suggested contact lenses. He'd worn them all through high school and college, but then he'd lost one, and money had been tight, so he'd gone back to an old pair of glasses. After the contact lenses she wanted him to buy a car. He'd tried to sell her on the charisma of a Harley, but she'd insisted that a motorcycle was cold, wet and impossible if you wanted to arrive somewhere looking like a person instead of a drowned rat.

Jack had let her rave on about all the things he should do to improve his situation when the money arrived. He planned to put the whole advance in the bank. Maybe, if he kept saving, he'd be able to quit his day job and write full time. Now, that would be heaven.

That and having Krysta near him full time. But that was truly out of reach, so he'd concentrate on the other goal and hope that in the chasing of it he'd ease the persistent, painfully sweet aché in his heart.

Two weeks had passed uneventfully when Krysta appeared once again on the shipping dock. This time she'd perched a yellow hard hat on her honey-blond

hair, and she wore a winter white pantsuit that defined
her trim figure beautifully. Jack threw the forklift into
neutral and sat there staring at her for the pure joy of it.
He must have been blind back in high school.

She walked over to the idling machine and tipped
her face up to look at him. Her gaze was anxious. "Can
I see you for a minute? We've got trouble."

Heart hammering, Jack glanced over at Bud and
held up his hand, fingers spread, to indicate he needed
a five-minute break.

Bud waved his approval.

Jack shut down the forklift and swung to the ground.
Trouble. Dammit, he'd known something would go
wrong with the book deal. Somebody had read the
manuscript and objected to any advance. He still had
no contract, and he wasn't sure what a verbal agreement was worth, especially if it came out that he hadn't
been the one agreeing.

Once again they headed for Bud's office. Jack held
the door for her, followed her inside and closed it se-
curely. "What kind of trouble?"

She faced him and took off the hard hat. She was
trembling. "I knew it was a mistake for me to pretend
to be you. I knew it from the beginning. I can't imagine
what we'll do now, Jack."

Her agitation required him to be the calming influ-
ence for a change. It was a nice change. He pushed
aside his own fears and placed both hands on her
shoulders. "Take it easy. We'll work it out, whatever it
is. Just tell me what happened."

She took an unsteady breath. "It was the picture.
They loved that picture. Before they got it they were

just going to announce the winner around Valentine's Day in some magazine I've never heard of."

"*Publisher's Weekly.* I know. It was in the contest rules."

"Well, now they want to do more. They want to make the announcement a big deal in New York on Valentine's Day, and, Jack, they want Candy to be there!"

"To be there?" Stunned, he released his grip on her shoulders. "You must have misunderstood. They don't treat first-time authors like that."

"That's exactly what Stephanie said! But they've re-vamped their plans, considering the picture, and the...bigger advance—"

"Aha!" He stabbed a finger in her direction. "*You* helped us get into this mess!"

"Jack, I had no idea this would happen." Her green gaze pleaded with him. "You'll have to tell them. You'll just have to tell them the truth."

He went cold at the prospect. They'd bought Candy Valentine as a package, a package that now included a beautiful, promotable author. Now they were planning a big reception in New York for their latest find, who'd had the guts to demand more money for her book.

He turned the matter over in his mind and could only come up with one solution. "I don't think it would be wise to tell them now," he said carefully.

"You have no choice!"

"Yes, I do." He gazed down at her. "If you'll help me."

She backed away as far as the little room would al-low. "Oh, no, you don't. I can't do this, Jack. Negotiating on the phone is one thing. Sending in my picture was okay, too, but I'm not—"

"Krysta, my career hangs in the balance." He was playing shamelessly on her caretaking nature, and he knew it. Later he might feel guilty. Right now he was desperate. "I'll coach you. You'll be great. I know you'll be great."

"If you think I can go to New York by myself and pretend that I'm the person who wrote that book, you're crazier than I thought you were!"

Necessity became the mother of invention. "You won't be alone. I'll go with you."

"They're offering one first-class plane ticket, one suite at the Marriott Marquis. It would be inappropriate to ask to bring a guest on a business trip like this."

"They'll never know I'm there."

"You'll hide?" Her shocked expression gradually gave way to a giggle of laughter. "Jack, what *are* you suggesting? This is real life, not one of your books."

Her laughter brought a smile to his lips. This disaster was beginning to show its more appealing side. "You said it was a suite, right? Plenty of room for me, and nobody at Manchester has to know. I'll be around to coach you before each meeting and debrief you when you come back." *And we'll be together in that room all night.* "It will work, Krysta."

"You're crazy." She shook her head, but a smile still played around her mouth.

He could tell she was intrigued by the novelty of the plan, so he added another inducement. "Ever been to New York?"

"Of course not. It's a very expensive place to visit."

"Well, I spent time there during those years I

knocked around the country. It's an exciting city. And it sounds as if Manchester is ready to lay Manhattan at your feet."

"No, *your* feet," she corrected him.

"*Our* feet, then. What do you say?"

"I don't know, Jack." She lowered her gaze to her clasped hands. "You'll have to give me some time to think about this."

"How long?"

She glanced up at him. "I told Stephanie I'd call her back tomorrow with an answer."

"And of course you know you can trust me to be a complete gentleman at all times." *Unless you beg me not to.*

"Oh, of course. That's no problem."

He wished she hadn't replied to that with such complete conviction. She obviously still thought of him as good old Jack. She had no idea what being a gentleman in this situation would cost him.

KRYSTA SETTLED INTO the leather luxury of a first-class airline seat and sipped a mimosa the flight attendant had given her soon after takeoff. The champagne and orange juice combination heightened her sense of unreality. It was difficult to believe she was on her way to New York, traveling in a style she'd only seen portrayed in the movies.

She'd told her father and brothers the same story as everyone else, that she'd won a free weekend at a health spa. They'd all been so happy for her she'd felt incredibly guilty about the lie, but she and Jack had agreed they couldn't chance letting anyone, not even her beloved family, know the truth.

Gazing out the window at the blanket of clouds below, she tried to appear nonchalant about the trip. Her every action would reflect on Jack's reputation, and she was determined to represent him to the best of her ability. Thank heaven no one occupied the seat next to her. She wasn't up to answering the kind of questions chance traveling companions often asked.

"Ms. Valentine?"

Krysta didn't respond.

"Excuse me, Ms. Valentine." The flight attendant touched her arm.

Krysta jumped before realizing that she hadn't answered to the name on her airline ticket. She'd have to work on that. "Sorry—" She looked at the attendant's name badge. "—Holly. I guess I was daydreaming."

The flight attendant leaned forward, her expression solicitous. "I promise not to interrupt you again, but I need to get your order for lunch. We have beef tenderloin or a very nice tuna filet."

"The tenderloin would be fine." She tried to sound patient and slightly bored, as if she were asked to make that sort of decision on a regular basis while cruising thirty thousand feet above the ground.

"Good choice." The flight attendant straightened and turned toward someone who was standing in the aisle beyond Krysta's line of vision. "May I help you?" she asked in an imperious tone.

Krysta leaned forward and saw that it was Jack standing there, a large envelope in his hand. The flight attendant looked ready to march him straight back to his seat in coach.

"It's okay, Holly." Krysta said. "I need to speak to this gentleman a moment."

Holly looked Jack up and down. He wore a corduroy blazer that had seen better days and was a little tight across the shoulders, a red flannel shirt, jeans and weathered running shoes. His dark hair was caught back with a rubber band and his glasses were still held together with tape.

Jack met her appraisal with a calm gaze. "I promise not to contaminate the area for long, Holly."

Holly flushed. "Oh, I didn't—"

"Hey, it's okay. I realize it's part of your job to keep those of us in steerage from penetrating the velvet curtain." Jack's devilish grin transformed him into quite a rakish character, in Krysta's opinion.

Holly's attitude shifted. She smiled back. "Take as long as you like," she murmured, and gave him a sidelong glance before returning to the galley.

Jack plopped into the empty seat next to Krysta. "What're you drinking?"

"A mimosa. Orange juice and—"

"I know what's in a mimosa." He stretched his long legs and worked his shoulders into the padded leather seat. "Not bad up here. Thanks for putting in the good word for me, or I'd have been tossed out on my ear."

Holly reappeared and gave Jack a brilliant smile. "Can I get you anything?"

Krysta stared at the flight attendant. Jack had made a conquest. Somehow Krysta hadn't pictured Jack as the conquering type, yet with one disarming smile he had Holly eating out of his hand. Or maybe it was the tight jacket that emphasized the breadth of his shoulders that had caught her attention, or the light in his blue eyes. But she was definitely interested. Krysta glanced over at Jack, who seemed oblivious to the effect he was having on the flight attendant.

"Nothing for me, thanks," he said. "I'll just deliver my package and be on my way."

Holly leaned closer to Jack. "No one's sitting there," she murmured. "As long as Ms. Valentine doesn't mind, I don't think it would hurt anything if you—"

"Highly inadvisable, Holly," Jack interrupted, his grin flashing again. "Disturbing the social order is a dangerous business. If people like me start infiltrating first class, next you'll find us storming executive dining rooms, then invading private clubs." He nudged his glasses back onto the bridge of his nose. "And before you know it—anarchy."

Holly laughed. "I hardly think so."

"Besides, I'm sure my seatmates miss me already." Jack handed Krysta the fat envelope he'd been holding. "In all the rush I forgot to give you some reading material for the trip."

"Oh!" Krysta took the package, which probably contained his manuscript. She'd asked to read it on the plane and then had forgotten her request. As he eased his large frame out of the seat and into the aisle, she glanced up at him. "What seatmates?"

"I think they said they were traveling to a beauty pageant or something."

"And I suppose you're in the middle seat?" His sudden transformation into Don Juan was quite irritating.

Amusement sparkled in his eyes. "It seemed like the gentlemanly thing to do. See you later...Ms. Valentine."

Krysta watched him stroll down the aisle and push aside the curtain dividing the first class cabin from coach. Then she became aware that Holly was also watching his departure.

"You know who he reminds me of?" Holly said.

"I really can't imagine."

"Clark Kent. I can just picture him whipping off those glasses and turning into Superman."

Krysta resented the dreamy expression on Holly's face, and the thought of Jack sandwiched between two beauty pageant entrants didn't improve her mood. "I'd like another mimosa, please, Holly," she said.

"MS. VALENTINE?"

Krysta left the page she was reading with great reluctance to look up at Holly. "What?"

"We'll be landing soon. I'll need to have you stow your tray table and return your seat to the upright position, please."

"Landing? In New York?"

"That's correct. We should be on the ground in four-teen minutes."

Krysta glanced at her watch, unable to believe that hours had passed while she'd been totally engrossed in Jack's book. She vaguely remembered cutting the tenderloin all up so she could feed herself with just her fork while she continued to read.

In those hours she'd become the characters in Jack's book, and through them she'd experienced anger, joy and sorrow. She still had two chapters to go, but already she'd been drawn into a love so deep it brought tears to her eyes. And in its wake she'd felt the characters' sexual desire, felt it with a visceral response that had left her restless and aroused. Stephanie's comments about Jack's love scenes hadn't prepared Krysta adequately for Jack's expertise in that area. Expertise on paper, Krysta reminded herself. Just because Jack could write about making love in such sensuous detail didn't mean that he'd be that kind of lover in real life.

Not that it mattered what kind of lover he was. Jack might have managed to finish a book and sell it, but deep down he still lacked the sort of drive and ambition that she sought in a man. His willingness to take a low advance was proof of that. She suspected he'd never be particularly concerned about how much money he made on his writing so long as someone continued to publish him.

Yet his ability with words intimidated her a little, truth be told. Talent like that didn't come along every day, although Jack was the sort of man who might squander his impressive talent. She'd do her level best to make sure that didn't happen in the next four days, at least, although it was a frightening responsibility now that she knew what Jack had to offer the world.

Derek's intellect had never frightened her, and he had never squandered a single opportunity in his upward journey, according to the tales he told. She admired that sort of drive, but she wondered if reading Jack's book might help Derek learn to kiss better. Jack's description of a long, lingering kiss had made her tingle as she read it. Her two personal experiences with kissing Jack hadn't been like that at all. The first had been her idea, and it had been over before either of them had quite realized what had happened. The second kiss had been more like a bomb detonating than the slow, sweet seduction Jack had written about so well.

Jack probably just had a good imagination, Krysta

thought as she handed her glass and crumpled napkin to Holly and stowed her tray table in the arm of the seat. He'd only created a fantasy, after all, she mused while gathering the pages together and returning them to the envelope. Real life could never live up to the sort of pleasure Jack had depicted between a man and a woman. Only a fool would think differently, and she was no fool.

She fastened the envelope's clasp and held the package on her lap as the plane descended. When the plane hit an air pocket she gripped the envelope with both hands in a sudden possessive gesture. It was, she thought as the plane's wheels skidded on the tarmac and the New York skyline appeared in miniature outside her window, a very good book.

JACK'S HEIGHT ALLOWED him to hand down parcels stored in the overhead bins to the two women who had sat on either side of him during the flight. While in Seattle for a genealogy convention, they'd loaded up on souvenirs for their respective grandchildren. After several hours of anecdotes and accordion-folded snapshot holders, Jack could recite the exact ages, names, hobbies and cute little habits of Sadie's six grandchildren and Bernice's five. He'd heard about Sadie's battle with gallstones and Bernice's recent knee operation. And he knew more than he'd ever cared to about the problems of menopause.

He'd been delighted with the nonstop conversation because it had kept his mind off the nerve-racking idea of Krysta sitting in first class reading his book. Sending it to New York hadn't taken as much courage as walking it up the aisle to the front of the plane. If she hated the book she probably wouldn't tell him, but he'd know, anyway. Her opinion meant more to him than he'd ever imagined it could when he'd proposed this crazy scheme, and he was really sweating her response.

At least he wouldn't have to face her immediately. First class would deplane ahead of coach, and all she'd brought was a rolling carry-on bag, so she'd be down the jetway and whisked off by a waiting limo driver before he made it into the terminal. He'd take a bus. Fortunately he knew his way around New York and could get to the Marriott Marquis using public transportation. To say he was on a budget this trip was a gross understatement.

Knowing he was in no rush, he offered to help carry Bernice's and Sadie's packages, an offer they accepted after some protest. He blocked the aisle so they could climb out and then followed them, his duffel bag slung over one shoulder and a bulging shopping bag in each hand.

"You should come to my hairdresser in Brooklyn while you're here, Jack," Bernice said over her shoulder as the two women preceded him down the jetway. "I'll bet if you had a nice haircut, you'd be surprised how the girls would flock around."

"Thanks, Bernice. I'll consider it." Jack smiled to himself. Bernice seemed to have taken lessons from Krysta, except that Bernice's goal was to marry him off, not send him up the corporate ladder.

"I could get you a discount on a better pair of glasses," Sadie added. "That has to be uncomfortable, with the tape and all."

"I'm used to it, but thanks."

Outside the jetway two middle-aged men stood waiting and Bernice and Sadie rushed toward them, arms outstretched. Jack followed with the bags and was introduced to the husbands, each of whom clapped him on the back and invited him home for a good meal.

In the flurry of goodwill Jack almost missed seeing Krysta wander right past the limo driver holding a sign with "Candy Valentine" written on it. He glimpsed her mistake in time to excuse himself from the two couples and sprint after her.

"Candy!" he called.

Paying no attention to the name, she continued down the terminal pulling her rolling carry-on. He muttered a curse as he dodged through the crowd after her. They'd agreed not to use her real name here in New York so the publisher wouldn't be able to trace her in any way and discover discrepancies in her story.

Finally he got near enough to grab her arm. With a cry of alarm she swung her purse at his head.

He ducked. "Hey! It's me!"

"Jack!" Color drained from her face as she stood there trembling. "I thought you were a mugger."

"Sorry. Let's move out of the center of traffic." He propped his duffel bag on top of her suitcase and took command of the handle while he used his free hand to guide her away from the flow of people.

She leaned against the wall and put a hand to her chest. "Whew. Adrenaline rush."

"I didn't mean to scare you, but you missed the limo driver. He's back at the gate."

"I didn't see anyone."

"He was holding a sign that read Candy Valentine."

"Oh." She took a deep breath and gave him a sheepish smile. "I really should have practiced more with that name. That's twice I've spaced out about it."

"If you hurry, I'm sure you can catch him. It was a big plane, and I imagine people in the back rows are still getting off."

"But he probably saw me walk right past him. What will I say?"

"Tell him the truth. It's your new name and you still aren't quite used to it."

"I'll do that." She straightened and peered down the length of the terminal. "Can you see him from here?"

"Yeah. He's wearing a navy uniform and a billed cap, just like you'd imagine a proper chauffeur would."

"Where?" She stood on tiptoe.

"Over this way." Taking her by the shoulders, he pointed her in the right direction to see the chauffeur. Beneath the fabric of her suit jacket, her body felt warm and supple, and he caught a whiff of her delicate cologne.

"I see him now."

He released her with reluctance. "I'd better not walk down with you."

"That's okay. I'll be fine." She smiled at him. "Sorry to have tried to clobber you like that. It's just that I've heard all those horror stories about New York, and when somebody grabbed me, I reacted."

"Good. I'm glad you have that kind of reaction. You probably won't have any problems because you'll be with people all the time you're here, but it's a good idea to stay alert. The crime here doesn't match the reputation, but you still have to be reasonably careful."

"I will be." She gazed at him with a warmth that he found disconcerting. "I liked your book, by the way."

The book. Ah, yes, the book. He swallowed. "You did?"

"Yes. You're quite a lover on paper, Jack. See you at the Marriott." She turned and walked toward the uniformed chauffeur.

Jack stared after her, his heart pounding. One thing was for sure. Krysta Lueckenhoff could deliver a hell of an exit line.

5

WHEN KRYSTA WALKED through the door of the suite it took real effort to stifle a gasp of pleasure.

"I trust this will be satisfactory," the bellhop said as he wheeled her suitcase through the door.

"It will be fine," she said.

"Would you like me to unpack your things?"

"No, thank you." She extended her hand with the folded bill she'd decided on for the tip. She hoped it was enough.

The bellhop took the money and smiled. "Thank you. Enjoy your stay."

After he left, she gave him some time to walk down the hall before she let out a whoop of delight and spun around in the center of the room. Then she approached the floor-to-ceiling windows carefully, her stomach churning, both from the thought of being so high above the city and the excitement of a wide-angle view of Times Square. Just as Jack had predicted, Manhattan lay, literally, at her feet. She'd give anything if her father and brothers could see this. Joe, especially, would go crazy. But she didn't dare even take pictures, because she was supposed to be at a health resort.

She'd been reading travel guides for days in preparation, but to actually see the band of illuminated news parading around the top of the triangular Allied Tower gave her goose-bumps. Chips of light dotted skyscrapers as office switches were thrown to greet the approaching night. Krysta's gaze swept outward, and the chips became sparkling pinpoints that finally blended into a dazzling necklace of gems stretching to the horizon.

The faint bleat of taxicabs drifted up from the streaming activity on the rush-hour-filled streets, but Krysta felt wrapped in the serene isolation of privilege. On the forty-fifth floor she smelled no carbon monoxide, only the fragrance of a huge bouquet of flowers sitting in the center of a banquet table placed near the suite's wet bar.

She wandered over to the bouquet, so big she couldn't get both arms around it. The card read, "Welcome to the Big Apple, Candy. Manchester Publishing."

So Jack's publisher had arranged for the bouquet. The gesture reminded Krysta that she wasn't here on vacation. Tomorrow morning Stephanie Briggs would be waiting in her office for the arrival of Candy Valentine. The reality of what she was attempting slashed Krysta's fantasy balloon to ribbons.

For the next three days she was supposed to be romance novelist Candy Valentine, an author with impressive skills, and she'd never written anything more creative than a personal letter. The people at Manchester Publishing would see through her facade immediately. She'd end up embarrassing herself and ruining Jack's career before it even got started. This was the dumbest stunt she'd ever tried. If she was smart she'd—

The sound of the telephone made her jump. The ring seemed to be coming from everywhere, but she located a phone next to a flowered sofa. She crossed over to it, then hesitated with her hand over the receiver. It could be Stephanie from Manchester. Answering the phone would commit her to this charade, once and for all.

She walked away from the phone and into the bedroom, which had no windows but was lit softly by bedside lamps flanking the broad expanse of a king-sized bed. The phone next to the bed was also ringing, and a third ring seemed to be coming from the bathroom.

She investigated, and sure enough, there was a phone in there, too. As she gazed at it, all the phones stopped ringing. She let out a sigh of relief and walked into the bedroom to sit on the edge of the bed and think.

Within thirty seconds the ringing started again.

"Oh, all right!" She grabbed the receiver, figuring she could always pretend to be very sick. In fact, that was an excellent plan. She made her voice sound low and throaty. "Hello?"

"Krysta? Where the hell have you been? And why do you sound like one of the Budweiser frogs?"

"Oh, *Jack.* I thought you were Stephanie. I was pretending to be sick."

"What on earth for?"

"I—I'm getting cold feet, Jack."

"Is that why you let the phone ring about twenty times without answering before?"

"Was that you, too?"

"Yes, that was me, and as the phone kept ringing I pictured you passed out, tied up, murdered by the bellhop, you name it. I can't decide whether I'm mad as hell that you're okay or faint with relief. Anyway, I'm glad nothing's wrong."

"Something *is* wrong. I can't do this. I don't know anything about writing, and I can't possibly—"

"Give me the room number so I can come up."

"Okay, but I'm warning you that we might as well call Manchester right now and confess everything."

"What's the room number, Krysta?"

She told him.

"Be right there."

While she waited for him, she paced and rehearsed a speech about honesty being the best policy. Finally, a firm knock sounded on the hall door, and she checked through the peephole before opening it. Her speech was on the tip of her tongue, but when he walked in, his expression a mixture of hope and determination, she couldn't say a word. He was counting on her to come through for him, and she couldn't let him down, no matter how scared she was.

"You okay now?" he asked, looking into her eyes.

"I'm okay."

"Good. I know you can do this."

She felt ashamed of her momentary loss of confidence. Jack didn't need her to fall apart on him, and she vowed not to do it again. "Can you believe this place?" she asked.

He surveyed the luxurious suite. "Wow. This isn't bad." He dropped his duffel bag in the middle of the room and crossed to the windows. "Not bad at all. I would say Manchester thinks a lot of Candy Valentine."

"Definitely." She gestured toward the flowers. "Those are from them, too."

"No kidding?" He went over to inspect the bouquet and read the card. "Very classy," he remarked, tucking the card back inside the arrangement. Then he glanced at Krysta. "You look right at home here, you know. I guess suites at the Marriott are your style."

"I've never stayed in a place like this in my life."

"Stick with Derek Hamilton and it'll probably be one fancy hotel after another."

Before she could stop herself, Krysta grimaced at the thought.

Jack's eyebrows lifted. "Do I detect trouble in paradise?"

She turned away from his perceptive gaze and walked toward the windows.

"Come on, Krysta." Jack walked over to join her by the windows. "You can tell old Jack."

She sighed. It would be nice to confide in someone. She hadn't dared tell even Rosie about her aversion to becoming intimate with Derek. But after reading Jack's manuscript, Krysta had an idea that he'd understand. She concentrated on the news flashing around the Allied Tower's perimeter. "Derek is the perfect sort of man for me," she began. "He's going places and he can help me go places, too."

"I absolutely agree. So what's with the sour face when I mention the very same thing?"

"I...don't like kissing him. And if I don't like that part, I can't imagine I'll like...the rest," she admitted softly. When Jack didn't respond to her statement, she glanced sideways at him. "Did you hear what I said?"

He stared straight ahead, his hands jammed in his jeans pockets. "Uh-huh."

"Do you think that's a legitimate problem?"

His stance didn't change. "Sure."

"What do you think I should do about it?"

He turned to her slowly, his hands still in his pockets, his eyes hooded. "I haven't the slightest idea."

She felt disappointed. Jack was no help at all. "Maybe I'm being too picky. I mean, it's not as if real life can be as romantic as your kiss-in-the-rain scene, for example."

A subtle change came over his expression and a soft light grew in his eyes. "You could try dragging Hamilton out in the rain and find out."

"Oh, Jack, be serious."

"This is as serious as I get."

"In the first place, I can't picture Derek standing in the rain without an umbrella."

The corners of his mouth twitched. "Well, now, that's a damned shame."

"You *are* making fun of this, aren't you. I should never have—"

"Of course you should have. That's what friends are for. I'll give this some thought, I promise, and get back to you on it. Now, shall we unpack?"

"Okay." She started toward her suitcase and paused to look back at him. "I don't want you to think there's anything *wrong* with Derek. I'm sure, with some help, that he could improve his technique."

When Jack just gazed at her, she put both hands on her hips. "What?"

"Maybe it's not Derek at all. Maybe it's you."

Chagrin heated her cheeks. "Well! That was certainly blunt."

"I didn't mean that you weren't good at kissing or making love," he said more gently. "I meant that you're just not attracted to him. No matter what he did, it wouldn't be exciting to you."

"Oh." Her wounded ego began to recover. "I've thought of that, but why wouldn't I be attracted to him? He's good-looking, ambitious, clever and polite."

"You sound as if you're placing an order in a catalogue. I'm sure you know love doesn't work that way."

"There's nothing wrong with having a list of qualities you want in a man."

"Not if you understand yourself well enough to know which qualities you need."

She really didn't care for his tone. "Well, I do, and if you put it that way, then kissing isn't really that important."

"Not if you don't think so."

"Honestly, I don't. Not really. It's a small problem. I shouldn't have brought it up in the first place." She grabbed the handle of her suitcase and without thinking started toward the bedroom. Then she realized that she couldn't just appropriate the bed, especially considering the suite was more for Jack than for her.

She turned back and gestured toward the bedroom doorway. "You can have the bed, if you want, and I'll take the couch."

"No. I asked you to come along. The bedroom's yours."

"But I'll get all those meals meant for you, and the night out at the theater, and heaven knows what else. Besides, it's a king-size and you're too tall to be comfortable on the couch. You take the bed."

"Want to flip for it?"

She gazed at him and smiled. She did enjoy this playfulness of Jack's. "Okay."

He fished a coin from his pocket. "Winner gets the

bedroom, loser bunks on the couch." He spun the coin upward. "Call it."

"Heads."

Jack caught the coin and slapped it on the back of his hand. Then he looked up at her. "You win."

"Really? Let me see."

He pocketed the coin. "You doubt my word?"

She did, as a matter of fact. When the coin was in the air, she'd had a premonition Jack would make sure she won the toss. "Thanks, Jack."

"You're welcome. For my next trick I'll buy you dinner."

"That's not necessary. I have money to—"

"Manchester suggested that Candy order room service tonight, remember? And get rested up for the big day tomorrow."

Krysta laughed. "I had forgotten Manchester would be paying. I accept your offer. Go ahead and order whatever sounds filling that we can share while I change into something more comfortable."

JACK WISHED KRYSTA hadn't phrased it quite that way, which presented images of her reappearing in a revealing negligee, leaning seductively in the open bedroom doorway and crooking one manicured finger in his direction. Sometimes his active imagination was a curse. He didn't even want to see the king-size bed she'd mentioned.

He tossed his duffel bag into a spare closet next to the wet bar and hung his sport coat in there, too. Then he located the room service menu.

So she hadn't slept with Hamilton yet, he thought as he perused the menu. He probably shouldn't take any solace from that, because she still seemed determined to fashion Hamilton into the ideal mate for her. With her determination, she might succeed, especially if she was willing to settle for adequate lovemaking, as opposed to the kind capable of toppling a kingdom or beggaring a prince. Jack had never experienced that kind of passion, either, but he'd flirted with the possibility a couple of times, and he definitely believed it existed.

He had the receiver in his hand and was about to dial room service when he remembered that Candy would have to do it. Maybe it was an unnecessary precaution, but he'd rather not take a chance on any members of the staff discovering there was a man staying in Candy Valentine's room.

He crossed to the closed bedroom door and rapped on it. "You'll have to call in the order, Candy, my sweet." He figured she'd think the endearment was a joke, so he could get away with it.

She opened the door, her hair mussed from pulling on a powder blue sweatshirt that matched the sweat pants she wore. Her feet were bare. She looked up at him, her face pink and glowing after being scrubbed free of makeup. "Candy, my sweet," she repeated, rolling her eyes. "Really, Jack."

He shrugged.

"But you're right," she said, moving past him into the living room. "And when the meal arrives you'll have to hide, just like in those situation comedies."

He'd imagined her coming out in a negligee, but somehow her casual attitude at sharing this suite, along with her mussed hair and her bare feet, had nearly the same effect on him. She seemed so damned relaxed and approachable that he wondered what would happen if he just walked over to her and took her in his arms. He already knew how she wanted to be kissed. Hell, he'd written the book on it.

She reached for the telephone and pulled her hair behind her ear as she placed the receiver over it. "What are we having?"

He noticed she'd taken off her earrings, her watch, and the rings she wore. *At home with Krysta.* God, it was an appealing thought. "Seafood pasta, a large spinach salad and a bottle of Pouilly-Fuissé," he said.

She turned, the phone still to her ear, and stared at him. "That's very *good*, Jack. I didn't think you had it in you to eat food like that."

"The pasta and spinach salad are for you and the wine's for me."

"Oh, no, you don't. We have to review our strategy tonight. I want you fed and sober."

He'd settle for just having her want him, period. "I think we deserve the wine. We don't have to drink much of it." Come to think of it, he might be forced to finish off the bottle after she went to sleep. His writing schedule had turned him into a night person, and he might need the sedative effects of the wine to counteract his normal schedule, not to mention the added stimulation of having Krysta in the next room all night.

She punched in the number for room service. "All right. I'll order the wine, but I'm monitoring how much you drink. I need to be fully briefed before I head out tomorrow. I haven't even finished—" She paused and returned her attention to the telephone. "Hello? This is Kr—, uh, Candy Valentine. I'd like to order dinner, please."

After ordering, Krysta went back to the bedroom to finish unpacking and Jack pulled the proposal for his second book out of his duffel bag to look it over. After the reception for his first book, he figured he should feel confident about this second idea, but he didn't. Krysta would be his first reader, and he was more than a little nervous about her reaction.

Krysta came back out of the bedroom just as the knock sounded on the door. "Quick, into the bedroom," she whispered.

"I wonder if this is what a married woman's lover feels like," he murmured as he walked past her.

"It speaks well of your character that you have to ask. Now get in there and close the door. Don't come out until I come to get you."

"Yes, ma'am." He followed her instructions and shut himself inside the bedroom. The scent of her cologne assaulted him immediately, and he closed his eyes and breathed deeply. When he opened his eyes, the first thing he saw was a huge bed that teased him with all sorts of possibilities. Worse yet, she'd tossed a flowered nightie across the pillow. It didn't surprise him that super organized Krysta laid out her night things when she unpacked, but it certainly unnerved him.

Knowing it was a terrible mistake, he walked over to the bed and ran a hand over the nightie. The yellow-and-white daisies suited her personality, and the softness of the material hinted at a sensuality that he'd suspected for some time. Hamilton wouldn't make her happy. Not in bed, anyway. Jack wasn't sure enough of himself to think he could, either, but he'd give anything to be allowed to try.

He glanced into the bathroom at the array of lotions and potions she'd arranged in a neat row. He'd always been fascinated by women's beauty routines and aroused by the myriad cosmetics they employed to make their soft bodies even more enticing. Leaning against the doorjamb, he allowed himself to fantasize what it would be like if he and Krysta were here as vacationing lovers instead of being involved in this crazy plot to pass him off as a woman writer. The thought made him ache with longing.

"Jack?" Krysta opened the bedroom door. "I'm sorry. I swear that was the slowest waiter in the world, but he's finally gone. You must have been bored stiff waiting around in there."

He pushed himself away from the doorjamb. Little did she know. And that's probably the way he'd be wise to keep it if he didn't want to face big-time rejection. "Actually, I've been trying on your underwear."

She rolled her eyes. "Someday that wise-cracking tongue of yours is going to get you into big trouble, mister. Let's eat. I'm starving."

So was he, and the seafood pasta tasted far better than he'd expected. Maybe there was more to life than Cheetos and Milk Duds, after all. Even the spinach salad wasn't half bad.

He speared a few more leaves onto his fork. "I'm getting into this green Popeye stuff," he said.

"It's the dressing. I take it you don't cook."

"Sure I do." He stabbed a piece of shrimp from the plate they were sharing. "You should see me nuke a bag of popcorn. Nobody can touch me in that department."

"Popcorn's not as bad as some of the things I've seen

you eat. It's a wonder you keep going, a guy as big as you are, with the type of things you put into your body."

"I have a highly efficient metabolism." He poured himself another glass of the Pouilly-Fuissé and gazed at the panorama of lights outside the window. He'd forgotten how stimulating New York could be. Or maybe, just maybe, it was the company that made the difference. He lifted the glass to his lips.

"You'd better take it easy on the sauce, Killigan. Don't forget you're using a water glass, not a wine goblet. The glass holds more."

"So do I."

She sighed and shook her head. "I can see you're going to be difficult. We'd better go over your new proposal now before your thinking gets too muddled."

"Does your thinking ever get muddled, Krysta?"

She gave him a long look. "In what way?"

"You always seem so in charge of everything, so sure of your direction." He swirled the wine in his water glass and took another swig. "I just wondered if you ever get confused."

Her gaze became wistful. "I guess I never thought I had that luxury."

"Everyone has that luxury. It's called being human."

Her answering sigh revealed more than she might have intended. "Oh, I'm human, all right. Sometimes I just feel like saying to hell with everything and running away to raise flowers or something."

He decided to pursue it. Maybe the wine had loosened her up a little bit, too. "And why don't you?"

She stared into her wineglass. "Because I'm afraid they'd all fall apart without me," she said softly.

"Your brothers?"

She nodded. "And Dad. He'll need a full-time nurse in the fall, when Joe goes away to college. That's why I've been trying so hard to get this promotion, so there would be enough money to pay for that."

"Krysta, your brothers are all good guys. I can't believe they expect you to take on that burden alone when you can't really afford it."

"You're right. So I've led them to believe I can afford it. That way, they won't be tempted to drop out of school to help pay."

He started to object to such self-sacrifice.

"Don't say it. I've heard it all from Rosie a dozen times. But you see..." She paused and gazed out the window. "How my mother would have loved this view."

"You still miss her."

"I think of her almost every day. She had such high hopes for all of us. One night when she was very sick, I got up for a drink of water and I overheard her tell my dad that they should have taken out life insurance on her so there would be money for everyone's college tuition. That's when I knew she would die."

His throat constricted. He dared not reach out for her and risk breaking the mood. She probably didn't let many people see this side of her.

"When I'd cried myself out that night, I made a silent promise to her that I'd see to it, that I'd get the boys educated. I knew with my dad's problems he wouldn't have the means."

"But you would."

She faced him, her gaze calm. "I have, and I will."

His inability to help filled him with frustration. It

was such a heavy responsibility for one young woman. Not that she couldn't do it. But the price might be very high. "Hamilton can greatly affect whether you get that promotion, I guess."

"You'd better believe it. If I hadn't agreed to go out with him in the first place, it wouldn't be so awkward. But we've been dating for several months now, and naturally he expects..."

"You deserve better." He knew it was the wine talking, but the wine spoke with more truth than he dared.

"I don't know how you can say that, Jack. He's an educated man with a bright future. He'd do anything for me."

"As long as you do one little favor for him."

"Watch it, Jack. I certainly don't think in those terms, and I'm quite sure Derek doesn't, either. But the reality is that I've indicated an interest and accepted his invitations, and now the reasonable thing would be—"

"To pay up?"

Her green eyes flashed. "That's enough. I will not have to go to bed with him to pay for the attention he's given me or to get that promotion."

He hated the thought that Hamilton had so much power to grant or crush her dream. "I hope you're right, but we're living in an imperfect world, with imperfect people, and you'd be naive not to consider that it might be his price."

She glared at him, obviously ticked off. "You are a very maddening person, Jack."

He leaned forward, nose-to-nose with her. He longed to take her in his arms and vow to protect her from the world, but he wasn't sure what that vow would be worth at the moment. "That goes double for you, Krysta."

KRYSTA MET JACK'S challenging stare as long as she could. He had a real knack for getting past her defenses, and there was no question that she was becoming attracted to him. Maybe it was because they'd just been discussing her potential sexual relationship with Derek, but she couldn't help thinking about the love scenes she'd read on the plane and wondering if Jack would be that kind of lover. Probably not. No man could live up to the idealized picture he'd painted. And yet, he'd written it, so he might come very close....

No. Jack might be attracting her on a physical level, but she had to stay focused on her goals, and his lack of drive would eventually erode any transitory pleasure of two bodies meeting.

"More wine?" he said.

"No, thank you." She forced her gaze away from his. She had a job to do. "Let's go over our plan for tomorrow and then I'd like to take a look at your new book proposal."

"Maybe we should forget about the proposal on this trip. You can say it's not quite ready, and I can mail it to them later."

"But it is ready, isn't it?"

Suddenly he looked very vulnerable. "I don't know."

"Let me see it," she said gently.

"I think it would be better if I reworked it after we get back. Then I'll just send it—"

"Give me your proposal, Jack." She held out her hand.

He slipped from his chair, took her hand and dropped to one knee. "Marry me, Krysta. I know I haven't much to offer except a kiss in the rain, but—"

"Oh, for heaven's sake." She jerked her hand away before he could tell that it had started trembling. *A kiss in the rain*. She'd begun to daydream about the magic of such a kiss, about making love to Jack. A marriage proposal, even in jest, set her pulse racing. "You're impossible," she said, grabbing the dishes and stacking them on the room service tray. "I want those pages and I want them now."

He stood. "If you get the pages, I get the Pouilly-Fuissé."

"No, you don't." She picked up the bottle and carried it over to the couch. "After we've finished with business, we'll see about the rest of this wine."

He crossed to an end table beside the couch and picked up a stack of papers. "Now I understand why your brothers called you *Sarge*."

She hid her agitation in the only way she knew, by taking on an air of brisk efficiency. "And they quickly learned that discipline was the key to success. I'm sure you know that, Jack. You stayed up all night to write."

"You don't understand." He held the book outline, reluctant to give it up. "I sacrificed sleep out of love, not discipline. I didn't force myself to write. It forced me."

She was taken aback by the statement. "Is that really true?"

He held up two fingers. "Scout's honor."

"I've never felt like that." She didn't minimize the significance of such an admission. He was obviously born to do this. "I envy you."

"Nevertheless, what I've produced while under that need to create can still be crap, you know."

"I seriously doubt it." She held out her hand again. "Give it here, Jack."

"Okay, and while you read, I'll just step out to the window ledge. If you don't like it, tap on the window and I'll jump."

"I am *sure* it's wonderful." She practically wrested the papers from his grasp, took them over to the couch and sat down to read.

Titled *Primary Needs*, the story was about a woman raised in foster homes and a politician who had much to learn about those less fortunate than he. In the beginning they squared off as enemies, but the groundwork was laid for them to become friends, lovers, and then enemies again when election time came and the issue of social welfare came between them.

Although she was engrossed in the story, Krysta finally became distracted by the steady rhythm of Jack's feet as he paced the floor in front of her. She glanced up. "Go do something."

"Like what?"

"I don't know. Do you have a deck of cards?"

"No."

"Well, you can't watch TV. That would bother me even more."

"I could take a walk," he suggested.

"That's silly. I don't have that much more to read. But you're driving me crazy pacing like that."

"I'll take a shower," he muttered, and retreated to the bedroom.

A moment later the water started, and with a sigh Krysta relaxed against the cushions of the couch and continued her reading. The story was, as she'd imagined it would be, wonderful. Even within this outline he'd captured the characters so well that she could see them in detail and hear the way they moved and talked.

More than that, she could see how they would come to love each other, both emotionally and physically. It was an explosive combination. Jack deserved even more money for this book, but she decided not to tell him that yet after the way he'd reacted to her last round of negotiating.

She picked up the outline and tapped it into shape again before heading for the bathroom.

Jack was just coming out, a towel wrapped around his waist and droplets of water still clinging to his mat of dark chest hair.

"The proposal's terrific," she said, thinking of nothing but the need to reassure him. After living with five men for most of her life, a towel-draped man was nothing out of the ordinary, anyway.

"You really think so?"

"Yes. The story has the potential to be even better than your last book, and I already told you how much I liked that one."

"God, Krysta, you don't know what that means to me." His smile flashed.

The brilliance of that smile shifted Krysta's attention dramatically. In the space of a few seconds, she forgot all about Jack's writing as she finally registered the sight of broad muscled shoulders, a flat stomach and lean hips that barely held up the towel Jack had knotted around his waist. He'd laid aside his glasses, and his long hair looked quite appropriate on a man dressed in something resembling a loincloth.

At the beginning of this escapade, she'd kidded herself that she'd be sharing a hotel room with good old Jack, a guy she knew so well he'd become nearly invisible. Well, he was invisible no longer. Not only was her roommate the most intelligent, gifted man she'd ever known, he was also a hunk.

Glancing away from the Adonis standing before her, she focused on the proposal in her hand. "I f-found a typo on page two." She fumbled with the paper and pulled out the offending page.

"You did? I went over it several times."

She realized her tactical error when he walked around to peer over her shoulder at the manuscript.

The fragrance of clean male filled her senses as he leaned closer. "Where?"

"You've spelled the word *passion* with only one *s*." Out of all the words he could have mistyped, it had to be that one.

"Guess I'll have to correct it in pen." His breath caressed her cheek.

She swallowed. This was ridiculous. Her heart was beating frantically, yet it was only Jack standing close to her. "Or I could find out if the hotel has a computer we can borrow." Doggone it, there was a definite quiver in her voice.

"Too much trouble. You'd better fix it, so it'll be consistent in case you end up having to write out anything else while we're here."

"I'll take care of it right now." She moved away from him and headed into the living room.

He followed her. "Use a black pen. I don't like the look of blue on a manuscript."

She glanced back at him. She had to get him to put some clothes on, and fast. "The curtains are open, Jack."

"So what? We're forty-five floors up."

She gazed at him, unable to come up with another excuse, yet unwilling to confess the truth—that his towel-clad body was giving her ideas she had no business having. Didn't *want* to have, under the circumstances.

Apparently she didn't have to say anything. Gradually, awareness dawned in his expression, along with a slow smile of male satisfaction. "I'll get dressed," he said, walking over to the closet and taking his duffel bag out. "And thanks, Krysta."

"For what?"

"For noticing me."

"Jack, I've always—"

"Not like that," he said quietly. Then he walked into the bedroom and shut the door.

JACK DECIDED NOT TO PUSH his luck. And luck seemed to be what he was having. He'd decided on a shower as a last-ditch distraction while Krysta finished reading his proposal. He'd thought about taking one earlier because he'd felt grubby after the bus ride to the hotel, so it seemed like killing two birds with one stone to take one while Krysta was reading his proposal. She had surprised the heck out of him by walking right into the bathroom, but he'd figured that was even more evidence that she didn't think of him in sexual terms.

And she probably hadn't before that moment. But one thing was sure. She did now. She probably wasn't too thrilled to realize she was physically attracted to him instead of to the guy she wanted to lust after, middle-management king Derek Hamilton. So Jack decided not to act on his newfound knowledge yet and see how Krysta would handle living with him for the next few days.

Consequently he was the perfect gentleman he'd promised to be while they had another glass of wine and talked about Candy Valentine's schedule for the next day.

"I'll give the proposal to Stephanie when I get to Manchester for the tour of the offices," Krysta said. Her bare feet were propped on the coffee table as she sat on the couch and sipped from her wine goblet. "That will give her maximum time to read it before Sunday morning, when we leave."

"I doubt if she will read it before we leave." Jack had chosen to sit in a club chair across from the couch. That didn't put him as close to Krysta as he would have liked, but he had the advantage of being able to study her when she wasn't looking. It was a luxury to record little details like the shade of pink she used on her toenails and the pattern of freckles across her nose, freckles that were usually covered by makeup and powder.

She crossed her ankles and scooted down lower on the couch. "I think she'll read it, and I think she'll make Candy an offer before we leave."

"Don't get your hopes up." Jack decided he liked her eyelashes better without mascara. There was a sweetness and vulnerability in her green eyes tonight. Then again, maybe that had nothing to do with the lack of makeup. He considered moving over to sit next to her on the couch but soon rejected the idea. No point in scaring her away just when she might be starting in his direction.

He picked up the typed schedule Stephanie had sent along with the airline tickets. "After the tour you're supposed to have a makeover. I'm not sure I like the sound of that."

She laughed. "It's a girl thing. We love makeovers."

"You wouldn't let them dye your hair or anything, would you?"

"I don't know. Would that be so terrible? Maybe I'd look great with ash-blond hair."

"What color is that?"

"Almost white, instead of this goldish brown I have."

He winced as he pictured her like that. The polished bronze of her hair was one of the things he treasured about her. "Don't let them change your hair color, okay?" He knew as soon as the words were out that they were far too revealing. "I mean, how would you explain that when we get back?"

"Everyone already thinks I'm at a health spa. They'll just consider the makeover as a part of it. Don't worry, I can cover my tracks."

Dammit, he liked her just the way she was. No telling what some New York salon would do to her. "But they were all crazy about that picture of you, so why would they want to change anything?"

"They probably liked the potential they saw in that

picture, but I'll bet they want a more sophisticated look."

"I think you're sophisticated enough." To hell with it. He'd beg, even if it did tell her too much. "Please don't let them bleach your hair lighter."

Her gaze was assessing. "Okay, I won't."

With a sigh of relief he went back to the typed schedule. "Good. So then you have a photo session, then a Broadway show, the exact one to be announced."

"Whatever they can wrangle tickets to, I guess. I'll be excited to go to anything on Broadway."

"It should be great," he agreed. "Then you have dinner at Sardi's." He glanced up. "Doesn't sound like I'll see much of you."

"Which is precisely why I'm taking the tote with the tape recorder in it, so I can replay all the comments for you when I get home."

"I wish you'd reconsider that. If somebody at Manchester discovers you're taping the conversations, it could blow the whole deal."

"Come on, Jack." She waved a hand in dismissal. "I can manage it. You agreed to it originally. You have to know the gist of the conversations to properly coach me on what else to say. I don't trust my memory to keep it all straight."

He knew she was right. "Okay, keep the tape recorder, but forget about smuggling food back to the room in that tote of yours. That's out."

"Don't be silly. I've heard about these five-course dinners at New York restaurants. I couldn't possibly eat it all. Don't you dare buy dinner. I'll bring you plenty, believe me."

"Don't do it, Krysta."

She got that smug little look on her face and he knew she had no intention of doing what he asked.

He resisted the urge to go over and kiss that smugness right away. "I can just imagine you coming back tomorrow night with pâté oozing out of the bottom of your tote bag."

She raised her eyebrows. "You know what pâté is? I'm impressed."

He rested his elbows on his knees and leaned toward her. "You seem to be under the impression that just because I don't eat exotic and health-filled items that I don't know what they are. I know all about them. I'd just rather have a hamburger and fries."

"You liked what we had tonight."

"Probably because I was starving to death." *Probably because you were there to share it with me.*

"Junk food is just a bad habit, Jack. If I were in charge of your diet for two weeks I'll bet you'd lose your taste for those things that are so harmful to your body."

He'd be willing to put her in charge of his diet for a lot longer than two weeks, but a few other stipulations would be included. He didn't think she was ready to hear about that. He reached for the nearly empty wine bottle. "Want to finish this off?"

"Actually, no. Considering the day I have ahead of me, I think I'd better get some sleep."

He pictured her going into the bedroom, taking off her sweat suit and slipping into the daisy-print nightie before climbing into the big bed and nestling under the covers. He could already tell it would be a very long night.

She stood and stretched. "Good night, Jack."

"Good night, Krysta."

She stopped in midstretch. "Oh! I need to loan you a pillow and blanket from the bed. I'll be right back."

He didn't have the heart to tell her it was wasted effort. He'd conditioned himself to function on very little sleep. Between his usual night-owl behavior and the stimulation of knowing Krysta would be in the next room, he'd be awake for hours.

"Here you go." She positioned the pillow at the end of the couch and arranged the bedspread over the cushions, tucking it in at the end with a practiced hand. She glanced over her shoulder at him. "Or would you rather I left this loose? Do you like to stick your feet out of the covers?"

Her endearing habit of caretaking really got to him. How he yearned to go over there, pull her down to the couch and show her how he'd really like to spend the night. "The way you have it is fine."

"I don't know." She stepped back, hands on her hips, to survey her handiwork. "This doesn't look very comfortable for a man your size. I think you should take the bed and let me sleep out here."

"It'll be fine. Besides, you're the one who has to represent me tomorrow. If anybody should get a good night's sleep, it's you. Can't have bags under Candy Valentine's eyes."

"I guess you have a point." She turned to him. "I brought some melatonin capsules for jet lag, if you want some to help you sleep."

"No, thanks. I'll be fine."

"I'll go get the bottle, in case you change your mind." She went into the bathroom and returned with a small plastic bottle. After shaking out a couple of tablets, she recapped the bottle and set it on the wet bar. "They're right here if you need them."

"Thanks, but I won't."

She sighed. "Sometimes it's so hard to help you out, Jack. By the way, what do you have planned for tomorrow? Obviously you can't stay in the room and let the maids see that you're staying here."

He laughed. It was so typical of her to worry about his day as well as her own. "Are you kidding? I wouldn't consider staying in a hotel room when I'm in the middle of one of the most exciting cities in the world. I'll be on the move all day, drinking it in."

"Gathering material for your work."

"You've got it."

A wistful look came into her eyes. "I wish I could go with you."

He met her gaze and allowed her to see a little of what he was feeling. Just a little. He'd hold off on the heavy-duty stuff for now. "I wish you could, too."

She didn't speak for several seconds. He could almost see the debate going on behind those green eyes. He was pretty sure she didn't want to walk into that bedroom alone any more than he wanted her to, but it would be a big leap for her to invite him to go with her. He didn't think she'd make that leap tonight.

She took a deep breath. "Good night, Jack."

"Good night, Krysta."

7

THANK GOODNESS she'd packed her melatonin to help her get a good night's rest, Krysta thought as her travel alarm beeped her awake. Jet lag might have messed up her sleep schedule, but not nearly as much as thinking about Jack would have. She'd never imagined that he could create such a hunger in her. Wanting to make love to Jack was definitely not part of the plan.

Fortunately such uncharacteristic behavior on her part could easily be explained by the unusual circumstances. First she'd read Jack's sensual manuscript on the way to New York. That had started her mind working in the wrong direction, and then she'd been stupid enough to walk in on him as he was coming out of the shower.

Probably most women would react the way she had, given that particular scenario. As long as she didn't read any more of Jack's work and gave him a wide berth when he was dressing or undressing, she'd be fine. She could go home to Derek with a clear conscience.

Well, almost clear. She'd had to tell him the same white lie she'd told everyone, about winning the health spa getaway contest. She and Jack had worked out every detail they could think of to protect the identity of Candy Valentine.

The only snag had been when they'd realized Manchester planned a photo shoot for a dust jacket picture. They both knew there was a chance someone might recognize Krysta when the book hit the stands. But after some thought they'd decided she could just laugh off any comments and put it down to a strange coincidence. The makeover would probably help, too. In Krysta's opinion, professional photographs seldom looked like the subject, anyway.

And that make-over and photograph session was today, Krysta reminded herself. She got out of bed and went over to the bedroom door to listen for some indication that Jack was awake. The total silence encouraged her to ease the door open and peek out.

Jack lay sprawled on his back on top of the bedspread, not underneath it as she'd anticipated. He still wore his jeans, but his flannel shirt was unbuttoned and askew, revealing the powerful chest that had unsettled her the night before. The steady rise and fall of that chest told her that he was still sound asleep.

His right arm trailed to the floor, where she could see one corner of a yellow legal tablet just beyond his outstretched fingers. So he'd found a way to write the night away, after all. A wave of tenderness engulfed her as she pictured him bent over his legal pad, totally engrossed in that magical world of creativity that inspired such wonder in her. She was so glad to have agreed to help him launch his career.

The legal tablet tantalized her with what it might contain, and despite her promise to herself, she was dying to find out what he'd composed while she slept. Perhaps he'd been working on *Primary Needs*. The story had captured her imagination, and it would be a thrilling treat to read the work as it came straight from Jack's mind.

He looked dead to the world. No doubt he'd kept his same schedule and had stayed up until early morning writing. She didn't want to disturb his much-needed rest, but a bomb would hardly wake him, from the looks of him.

Moving with great stealth, she crept out of the bedroom and around the coffee table to where the legal tablet lay. Sure enough, the top sheet was covered with Jack's bold script. He'd tossed his pen onto the carpet next to the tablet.

Sinking quietly to a cross-legged position, Krysta picked up the tablet and began to read. It quickly became obvious to her that Jack had been writing a love scene between the hero and heroine of *Primary Needs*. Krysta knew if she had any sense at all she'd replace the tablet and go take a shower—a very cold shower. She kept reading.

The politician had arrived unexpectedly at the home of the heroine, who was already dressed for bed and had pulled on a robe over her nightgown to answer the door. Inevitably, the politician took off the robe, and Krysta gasped. The heroine was wearing a soft nightie covered in daisies.

Just then a viselike grip surrounded her wrist, and her gaze lifted to meet Jack's.

His eyes were the color of a mountain lake, and just as cold-looking. "What are you doing?" His question rasped harshly in the stillness of the hotel room.

"I—I woke up, and looked out here, and—"

"That's mine." He took the tablet from her grasp and

tossed it on the coffee table. "No one sees it until I say so."

At first his tone chastened her, but she quickly recovered with a complaint of her own. "But I'm in there! Or at least, my nightgown is!"

He continued to hold her wrist in a manaclelike grip as he skewered her with his gaze. "Of course that seductive little nightgown is in there. People are always asking writers where they get their ideas. Well, now you know! Did you think I'd see it lying on your pillow and not use my imagination? Imagination is my stock in trade, Krysta."

"I just never thought—"

"Well, think." His grip tightened. "I never intended to spend the night counting sheep. After seeing that nightie I lay here in the wee small hours fantasizing about it, and you in it. And out of it. But what I wrote still belongs to me until I say different."

Her heart thundered and her vocal cords constricted, but she was determined to stand up for her rights. "You invaded my privacy with your words, but I'm not allowed to read what you've written until you say so? That's not fair, Jack."

"Maybe not." The night's growth of beard made him look dark and dangerous. "But writers have been revealing people's secrets for centuries and insisting on the autonomy to do it without censorship. It comes with the territory."

His unexpected aggressive behavior intimidated her, but it stirred something passionate in her, as well. She'd never considered that Jack possessed the dark and compelling sexuality he was displaying now.

She fought to keep her breathing steady. "Well,

you'll have to excuse me. I've never known a writer before." She glanced at his fingers still firmly clasping her
wrist. "You'd better let me go if you want me to be on
time for the limo."

Instantly he released her and lay back on the couch.
As she got to her feet and started to leave, he closed his
eyes and muttered a soft oath. "Krysta, I'm sorry. It's
just that I'm not used to—"

"I have to go." In her present state she was far better
off with his anger than his kindness. If he started being
sweet, no telling what sort of foolish behavior she'd in-
dulge in. She practically ran toward the safety of the
bedroom.

JACK TRIED TO APOLOGISE several times during the next
hour before Krysta left the suite, but he'd spooked her
and she wouldn't stay still long enough for him to
make amends. Finally, she whisked out the door, telling him she'd see him that night.

Once she was gone, he picked up the legal tablet and
threw it against the window. He'd definitely overreacted when he'd opened his eyes to see her reading his
rough—very rough, draft. Now that he'd adapted to a
computer, he was even more critical of anything he
composed on paper because a legal pad had no delete
key. Compared with his polished work, the scribblings
on the tablet seemed crude and embarrassing. Besides,
he wasn't used to having anyone around who might
chance upon his work before he was ready to have it
read.

But that didn't excuse his barking at her. Part of his
reaction had stemmed from his own guilt. He *had* invaded her privacy, and despite his defense of the prac-

tice, he was uneasy about it. The more he got to know Krysta, the less he wanted to reveal of her to the world. His nighttime writing effort had been more to relieve his frustration than to advance the action of his story. Yet he couldn't tell her that.

It was water under the bridge at this point, though. He couldn't stand there stewing about it forever when he needed to shave and vacate the room soon or risk having some maid discover him. While he was roaming the city today he might come up with a way to apologize that Krysta would be able to accept. He'd bragged about his tremendous imagination. Time to prove how good it was.

CARRYING HER TOTE BAG containing the tape recorder and Jack's proposal over one arm, Krysta entered the reception area of Manchester Publishing. It was smaller than she'd imagined, although a large brass version of the Manchester logo on one wall and numerous framed book covers left no doubt she was in the right place.

A young brunette with long permed hair and wire-rimmed glasses sat at the receptionist's desk. She smiled at Krysta. "May I help you?"

"Yes, I'm...Candy Valentine." Krysta had been practicing under her breath all the way over in the limo, but she still wasn't satisfied with her delivery.

The receptionist didn't seem to notice her hesitation. "Oh, Ms. Valentine! We've been expecting you. Have a seat and I'll tell Ms. Briggs that you're here." She picked up the telephone on her desk and punched a button.

Krysta sat in a sleek leather chair, reached into her tote bag and turned on the tape recorder.

The receptionist replaced the receiver. "She'll be right out. You know, you look exactly the way I pictured you would when I read your manuscript."

"You read Ja—my manuscript?" God, she'd have to be more careful. *She* was the writer now. It was *her* work, not Jack's, that she carried in the tote bag.

"My goal is to be promoted to editorial, so I offered to help read the Valentine's Day contest entries. I loved your story and sent it right to Ms. Briggs, along with a recommendation to publish." She looked very proud of herself. "My judgment was on the money, too."

"Then I have a lot to thank you for," Krysta said. She really didn't know much about this business, she thought. She'd imagined all manuscripts were read by editors, yet here was evidence that the first reader might just as easily be the receptionist in the outer office.

"Oh, no, I'm the grateful one. You should see some of the junk I've had to wade through. Your manuscript was a breath of fresh air. And *hot*, too." She winked at Krysta. "Just what I like."

Krysta managed a weak smile. She hadn't been allowed to finish the scene Jack had written the night before, but she had no doubt it had been steamy. And now she knew where he got his ideas.

"Besides that, my discovering you in the contest entries should be very good for my career."

"I'm glad."

"In fact, I'm keeping my fingers crossed that—" She stopped speaking as a tall woman in a gray wool suit walked into the reception area.

Krysta stood and was glad she'd worn three-inch heels. Otherwise Stephanie Briggs would have towered over her. From the cut of her slim suit to the casual perfection of her short brown hair and understated makeup, Stephanie was every inch the urban sophisticate. Krysta recognized a kindred spirit immediately.

"So you're Candy." Stephanie extended her hand. "I'm Stephanie."

"It's good to meet you at last." Krysta returned the firm handshake.

Stephanie's glance swept over Krysta and she smiled her approval. "It's even better to meet you and discover you didn't send us a twenty-year-old photograph. The marketing department will be very glad that you're as attractive as your picture."

Krysta thought about the inevitable day when the marketing department would learn that Candy Valentine was a man named Jack. "Are my looks really so important?"

"Ordinarily they're not. Most of our authors wouldn't make *People* magazine's list of the fifty most beautiful people in the world, and we really don't care. If you'd been homely, we still would have bought your manuscript."

"That's good to know."

"But we wouldn't have marketed the book, and you, the way we plan to under the circumstances. The fact that you're young and pretty is a publicity bonus, and we're going to make use of it. Now, come along, and I'll give you the fifty-cent tour of the place. The staff is dying to get a look at our next bestselling author."

As Krysta walked with Stephanie down the carpeted hallway she wondered how Jack would react to Stephanie's comments when he heard the tape. Viewing it from his perspective, he couldn't be very happy to learn that without Krysta, he might have been just another title on the rack instead of a highly promoted lead book. But she'd put the recorder in so that he'd know as much as possible about the plans for *Uptown Girl*, and he still needed that information even if some of it proved to be painful.

"I brought the proposal for my next book," Krysta said, lengthening her stride to keep up with Stephanie.

"Excellent. We need to start thinking about the book that will follow *Uptown Girl*. What's your premise?"

Feeling as if she were taking an oral exam, Krysta outlined Jack's story in a few sentences. Thank heavens she'd taken the community college public speaking course and knew how to present an idea.

Stephanie paused outside a doorway and faced her. "Good. Excellent. Do you have the outline with you?"

Krysta pulled the manila envelope containing the proposal out of her bag and handed it to Stephanie.

"I'll read it as soon as I can."

"Do you think you'll get to it before we—before I leave?" Krysta thought it would be best if she negotiated this next contract for Jack, too, and right now, she had the perfect opportunity to strike while the iron was hot.

Stephanie's eyes widened. "I can see you're not going to need an agent with business initiative like that. Yes, I'll try very hard to read it before you leave." She winked. "I can always go over a few pages between acts of the musical tonight."

"That would be great."

Stephanie laughed and took her arm. "You and I are going to make quite a team, Candy. Now come and meet the rest of the editorial staff."

As JACK CUT ACROSS to Fifth Avenue he realized he'd better have a terrific imagination if he intended to buy

Krysta an apology present on his limited budget. Zipping his ski jacket against a sharp winter wind, he shoved his hands in his pockets and started window shopping to get inspired.

Something to do with Valentine's Day, he thought as he passed displays dominated by red, white and pink. Not candy, especially with the obvious play on his new pseudonym. He liked to think he was more subtle than that. Flowers were a cliché, and besides, anything he could buy would look pretty sorry next to the bouquet provided by Manchester.

A trinket from Cartier, perhaps, or a tasteful leather item from Gucci. Sure. First he'd have to buy a few things for himself, like a ski mask and a water pistol. He'd never cared much about being rich, but walking down Fifth Avenue looking for a gift for Krysta, he would have loved to have unlimited funds.

Figuring there wasn't much point in going into Tiffany's, he bypassed it and headed for FAO Schwartz. Maybe whimsical could take the place of expensive. He hoped so.

Some time later he came out of the store with his purchase. The bag was small enough to stuff in his jacket pocket as he headed back down Fifth Avenue toward Brentano's. In Jack's opinion a walk through the streets of New York wasn't complete without a visit to at least one bookstore.

He planned to wander the aisles and dream of the day his book would be on sale. True, it wouldn't have his name on the cover, but it would be his story people were buying, his words they were devouring on the subways, during lunch breaks, at home in the evenings after the kids went to bed. Just thinking about that put an extra spring in his step.

Then, above the traffic noise, he heard a shout from somewhere ahead of him. A man dressed in dark clothes with a navy stocking cap pulled over his ears ran toward Jack, knocking pedestrians out of the way in his flight. A couple of people screamed and dodged out of the man's way.

Jack had no time to think, but his football training still ruled his instincts. Crouching down, he used his shoulders to throw the runner off balance. As the man spun around, Jack launched himself at his knees. They both went down with a thud on the cold cement, and Jack's glasses, not particularly secure in the best of circumstances, skidded across the sidewalk.

The man struggled, but working on the shipping dock had kept Jack in decent shape. He held the guy pinned to the sidewalk and called out for someone to get the police.

A squad car arrived at the same time as a well-dressed, portly man in a suit and topcoat trotted up, puffing.

As New York's finest took over and returned the wallet to the man in the topcoat, Jack got up and looked around for his glasses. It wasn't easy considering the view had become very fuzzy.

The man in the topcoat finished giving his statement to the police and walked over to Jack. "That was heroic, son," he said. "I'd just taken out my wallet to pay the cab driver when this fellow swooped in. I owe you a great deal for stopping him."

"Then maybe you could help me find my glasses," Jack said. "They fell off when I tackled him."

"Here they are," volunteered a woman, coming toward him with a mangled bit of plastic in her hand. "The lenses are smashed, I'm afraid."

The businessman stepped forward. "We'll take care of that in no time." He laid a hand on Jack's shoulder. "Come with me, my boy. My optometrist is excellent."

"Listen, I couldn't accept—"

"Nonsense. I had fifteen hundred dollars plus change in that wallet and the unlisted phone numbers of some very prominent people, not to mention credit cards and pictures of my grandchildren. I can't begin to imagine the mess I would have been in if you hadn't stopped that mugger."

"I'm glad I could help."

"You look like the type who would help out and then just disappear, like the Lone Ranger or something. I can't have that. I insist on replacing your glasses, at the very least." Without waiting for an answer, the businessman turned to hail a cab. "We'll pop on over to my optometrist's office right now."

"No, really. I'll just—"

As the cab pulled to the curb, the man glanced at Jack. "Listen, my wife will boil me in oil if she hears about this and discovers I didn't reward you in some fashion. Allow me to buy you new glasses and you'll save a forty-year marriage."

Jack decided further protest would make him seem ungrateful, so he followed the businessman into the cab.

Once they were moving through traffic, the man turned to him. "Now, don't take this amiss. I'm extremely grateful and I don't want to insult you in the least, but have you considered getting yourself a haircut?"

Jack leaned against the seat and grinned. "You sound like someone I know."

"Your mother, perhaps?"

"No, another...woman."

The man nodded. "It's up to you, of course, but my stylist is excellent, and it would be the least I could do. And as long as we're replacing those glasses, have you ever worn contacts?"

"Years ago."

"They've improved, believe me. I have the disposable kind, and they're a damn sight better than fooling with glasses. My optometrist could have them ready for you in twenty-four hours."

KRYSTA HAD WRANGLED two keys to the hotel room by convincing the front desk clerk that she was hopelessly absentminded and needed a second key to avoid locking herself out. If the front desk clerk on duty was suspicious, he hadn't indicated it.

By the time she returned to the room that night, she was exhausted. A Broadway baby she wasn't, if that meant arriving for work at nine and continuing to be bright and perky until after midnight. She didn't understand how Stephanie and the two men from marketing who had accompanied them to the theater and dinner managed to keep such a schedule. If today was a typical example, New Yorkers definitely lived a faster-paced life than people on the West Coast.

The living room was dimly lit with only one lamp burning, and Jack was already asleep on the couch. Krysta was just as glad. After the grueling day she'd had, she wasn't up to matching wits with Jack. Her defenses were down, and that wasn't a good position to be in with somebody who appealed to her the way Jack did. She deliberately avoided looking at him as she came in, so that she wouldn't be tempted to snuggle down beside him and let nature take its course.

Moving quietly around the suite, she opened the courtesy bar and took out several of the nonperishable items so that she could store part of what she'd been able to smuggle out of Sardi's. Jack should appreciate the chunk of prime rib she'd managed to wrap in a napkin. Red meat was his kind of treat, and she'd ordered the prime rib with him in mind.

She left the napkin-wrapped dinner rolls on the banquet table, along with a couple of pats of butter. She probably shouldn't have indulged his high cholesterol habit with the beef and butter, but this trip didn't seem like the time to take a dietary stand. She had more critical issues to hold the line on. Like staying out of Jack's bed.

The extra food put away, she took some melatonin from the bottle on the wet bar, snapped off the living room light and walked into her bedroom. Someone, probably Jack, had turned on the bedside lamp so she wouldn't have to stumble around in the dark. Very thoughtful. She yawned and went into the bathroom to take off her makeup.

There was a fair amount to take off. Before she started, she gazed at herself in the mirror. A high-priced hairdresser named Emilio had taken a good three inches off her hair and styled it differently. He'd told her he wanted to transform her from wholesome to seductive. According to Stephanie and the two guys from marketing, Emilio had succeeded.

The makeup session with Rudolfo had left her with thinner eyebrows, more hollow-looking cheeks and a pouting red mouth. In one of the photos she'd been asked to bite into a ripe strawberry, not necessarily to use for the jacket picture, but to get her in the mood, the photographer had said.

Krysta had spent the morning trying to imagine herself as an author. By the end of the afternoon, she felt like a *Playboy* centerfold. Jack's book seemed to be nearly forgotten in the frenzy to make the supposed author glamorous and sexy. One day down and two to go, she thought wearily. But it was all for a good cause, and she still felt good about the contribution she was making to Jack's career. With luck she wouldn't make any major mistakes as she played out this role.

With her face finally washed clean and her soft daisy nightgown on, Krysta returned to the bedroom, and for the first time saw that something was propped against her pillow. She slowly picked up a rounded plastic heart that fit easily in the palm of her hand.

The casing was decorated with a laser design that sparkled when she held it to the light, and the white-tipped shaft of an arrow protruded from one side. A folded sheet of yellow lined paper lay on the bed where the heart had been resting.

Putting down the heart, she unfolded the note. Jack's bold script greeted her.

Dear Krysta,
    I behaved in a heartless manner this morning. My heartfelt apologies.

                                        Jack

She picked up the heart again and examined it. An opening indicated that the arrow was designed to go all the way through. She pushed on the shaft, and the tip of the arrow slid through the other side at the same time that a message emerged from the top of the heart. *Be My Valentine.*

Her breath caught in her throat. *Oh, Jack.*

She pressed the little heart to her chest as the age-old message ran round and round in her head. She'd seen it hundreds of times today in her travels around the city, but the meaning had been obscured by the commercialism of the season. Now the phrase brimmed with meaning. And it demanded an answer that she didn't feel prepared to give.

8

JACK HAD BEEN AWAKE when Krysta had come home, but he'd deliberately played possum. He'd watched her through half-closed eyes as she'd puttered around the suite depositing the food she must have brought him from Sardi's.

The damned salon had cut her hair, which he would have vetoed if he'd had a vote. But there was something intriguing about the shorter style, too. It swung when she moved, drawing attention to the luster of her dark gold curls and giving her a sassy look he might even begin to like. Hell, who was he kidding? He'd probably find something to like if she'd shaved her head and put a ring through her nose.

The draw for him wasn't really her looks, although he enjoyed responding to that saucy smile and treasured gazing into her emerald eyes. It was her damned perseverance, her indomitable spirit, her optimism in the face of a challenge that squeezed his heart. He wanted to help shoulder her burdens, which was laughable considering he could barely shoulder his own at the moment. In point of fact, he'd had to ask her for help instead of giving it.

When she went into the bedroom, he listened intently for some reaction to his gift. Maybe she'd laugh. Maybe she'd wonder why he'd bother buying her such a cheap toy. Maybe he should have gone for a single rose, but that was Hamilton's sort of gesture, not his. Jack remembered seeing the rose on Krysta's desk the day she'd made the first call to Manchester. Nope, he didn't intend to follow in Hamilton's footsteps. Win or lose, and this was fast turning into a contest, he'd do it his way.

If he could write the end of this scene, Jack would have Krysta become so overwhelmed by the little plastic heart and its message that she'd walk back into the living room and softly call his name, just in case he wasn't sound asleep. Then he could pretend to wake up, and then...

He lay waiting, hearing nothing but Krysta's preparations for bed. Then the light went out. Bitter disappointment seared through him as he realized that his attempt to connect with her had failed miserably. He sat up in frustration and shoved his fingers through his hair. There was a hell of a lot less of it to shove his fingers through than there had been that morning. Krysta wasn't the only one who'd gotten shorn today.

He might as well admit he'd accepted the businessman's offer of a haircut because of Krysta. Not that she'd really care all that much, other than to be pleased that he'd decided to take more pride in his appearance. He ranked somewhere in the area of a project, a fixer-upper and nothing more. Her real focus was on somebody who didn't need any fixing, except for the minor imperfection of his kissing technique.

Which gave Jack an idea. It was an idea he had no right having, but his ego had become involved and was demanding he accept this challenge.

Krysta would be gone all the next day, too, but she had to come home sometime so they could go over the tapes she was making for him. And it was, after all, February 14, a day devoted to lovers. He'd noticed that the subject of kissing flustered her more than a little because it threw Hamilton into a bad light and made her wonder if Jack might not be a better bet in that department. Tomorrow night he'd reintroduce that volatile subject and see where it took them.

For a campaign like that, one he hadn't engaged in for some time, he wanted to be well rested. He should probably try to alter his body clock to be more of a match with Krysta's. He stood, walked over to the wet bar and picked up her bottle of melatonin pills. Tonight he would sleep.

As she showered and dressed the next morning Krysta decided she'd overreacted to the plastic heart. It was probably Jack's idea of a cute little joke, asking her to be his valentine. She had come on this trip to be his "Candy Valentine," so it probably was a play on that theme rather than a straightforward request for her affections. Sure, he'd wanted to make amends for snapping at her the way he had, but that was only because he still needed her to be his "Candy Valentine."

Still, Krysta wasn't positive about her conclusions, and she would have liked to have a few words with Jack before she left the suite. Consequently she'd made no effort to be quiet while she got ready for an eight-thirty appointment. She even made coffee in the pot located on the wet bar, thinking the gurgling and the scent would awaken Jack.

He didn't stir.

Finally, as she stood sipping her coffee, she walked over and stared down at him to make certain he was still breathing. That was when she noticed his hair. Her gasp of surprise had been enough to startle him awake the morning before, but today it had no effect. He slept on.

She evaluated the haircut as best she could, considering he lay on his side with his back to her. Whoever had done the job had a practiced enough hand to contour his hair to make the most of its natural wave, and the back feathered nicely to his nape. Although she'd counseled him to cut his hair, she was glad he hadn't asked the stylist to make it supershort. It wouldn't have suited his maverick personality to have the clipped, almost military cut of someone like...Derek.

Derek's haircut reflected his kissing style, now that she thought about it. Well mannered, brief and efficient.

Thinking of Derek's efficiency reminded Krysta that she had a limo to catch in ten minutes, and it didn't look as if she'd be having a conversation with Jack this morning. She returned to the bathroom to finish applying her makeup.

She was curious as to why he'd suddenly had his hair cut, and a little annoyed that he'd chosen New York as the place to do it when he could have found a much cheaper salon in Evergreen. That was pretty typical of Jack's impetuous behavior, though, and she probably shouldn't complain, because at least he'd done it. Funny, but now that he had, she almost wished she had his long hair back. Fresh from the shower and clad in a towel, he'd looked quite impressive with hair reaching to his broad shoulders.

There was also the question of why he'd had his hair cut yesterday. Maybe he'd done it out of boredom, from knocking around by himself all day, but that didn't sound like Jack. She doubted that Jack, with his fertile brain, was ever bored, which meant that he might have cut his hair for her. He might have bought the valentine heart as a sincere gesture instead of a cute joke. He might, just might, be making a play for her. The thought made her heart beat faster, but it didn't look as if she'd find out the truth about Jack's feelings this morning.

Three minutes before she had to walk out the door she checked her appearance in the full-length mirror at the far end of the bathroom. Before the photo shoot, Stephanie had taken her to a clothing rental shop to pick out the little red leather suit and white silk blouse she wore. Stephanie had said there would be some photo opportunities the next day along with the local talk show that afternoon, and Candy Valentine should definitely appear in red and white on February 14, of all days.

The skirt was shorter than Krysta would have chosen, but Stephanie had insisted on the outfit and proclaimed that Krysta looked as chic and sexy as a runway model. Krysta had pointed out that she wasn't as tall as a runway model and that discussion had led to Stephanie's confession that she'd once been a model. Krysta was enjoying the growing relationship with Jack's editor and regretted that it was built on a lie. She would have liked to keep Stephanie as a colleague.

Picking up the tote bag containing the tape recorder, a fresh supply of tapes and her coat, Krysta walked back into the living room and over to the couch. Leaning down, she shook Jack's shoulder. "Wake up, Jack.

I'm leaving now, and you'll have to vacate pretty soon, yourself."

He groaned and snuggled deeper into the pillow.

"Jack!" She shook him harder.

"Wanna sleep," he mumbled. "Having a good dream."

"Well, you need to get up. I'm leaving now, and the maid will be along any time."

Abruptly he turned over, his eyes wide open. "Krysta?"

"I'm sorry, Jack, but you have to get up. This is probably the first good night's sleep you've had in months, but we don't want the maid to find you here."

He gazed at her as a slow smile crept across his face. "Your stuff really works."

The shorter hair made a startling difference in his appearance. He looked far more cosmopolitan and worldly. She could imagine this version of Jack dining at Sardi's on paté. "What stuff?"

"That melatonin."

"So you finally took some. That was a good idea, Jack. Take some more tonight."

"I just might." His eyes glowed with a new intensity. "The dreams I had were incredible."

Belatedly, Krysta remembered one of the potential side effects of the herbal sleep aid—explicit sexual dreams. It hadn't happened to her, but apparently Jack was susceptible. Big surprise. Her cheeks warmed with embarrassment. "That sometimes happens with melatonin," she admitted. "I forgot to tell you about it."

"Too bad. I would have taken it sooner."

"Well..." She backed away from the sofa. "I really have to go."

"That's a shame." His gaze swept over her leather miniskirt and jacket. "Nice outfit."

"It's rented." Liquid fire ran through her at the look in his eyes.

"When will you be home?" he asked softly.

"I...I don't know." Her heart was beating furiously. He'd asked when she'd be *home*, not when she'd be back. The difference between the two closed them in an intimate circle.

"Any general idea?"

"Stephanie mentioned something about dinner, but I thought I might beg off."

The light in his eyes intensified.

"She and I will be going over the revisions for *Uptown Girl* this morning," Krysta hurried on, "and I'm sure you'd like to hear the tape of that."

"Yes, I would."

She backed away a few more steps. "I'll bet the limo's already down there waiting."

"Then, I'll see you tonight."

"Right. Oh, and I like your haircut."

"Same here."

"See you later." She turned and headed for the door.

"Krysta?"

"Yes?" She paused with one hand on the knob.

"Happy Valentine's Day."

She glanced around. It was a good thing people were counting on her to show up in a few minutes, she thought. Otherwise she would have turned around and run straight into Jack's arms, and that might be a very unwise move for both of them. "Same to you," she said, "and thank you for the sweet little heart." Then she walked out of the door.

THE BUSINESSMAN'S optometrist had loaned Jack some glasses to use until he picked up the contacts that afternoon. They were a major improvement over the taped ones he had been using. Once he was shaved and dressed he took note of the weather and discovered the sun was trying to break through. For the first morning in a long time, Jack was wide awake. After clearing away any evidence of his presence in the suite, he grabbed his jacket and legal tablet before setting out toward Central Park.

He found a vacant bench and sat down to people-watch and write descriptions of interesting passersby. Unfortunately, the only description he seemed able to write concerned a woman who was nowhere near Central Park, a woman who was currently sitting in Stephanie Briggs's office, a woman wearing a very sexy red leather suit.

His preoccupation pointed to a malady he wasn't ready to admit, so after a while he flipped the legal pad closed and walked over to the Metropolitan Museum of Art. Half an hour later he walked out again, disgusted with himself. The last time he'd visited New York he'd spent hours wandering through the exhibits and marveling at the sheer volume of creativity displayed there. This morning he'd spent the entire time musing in front of Rodin's bronze titled *The Kiss* and thinking about Krysta. He'd pretty much wasted the admission fee.

He couldn't see much point in going to the Museum of Natural History and wasting more money. Even the Statue of Liberty would probably remind him of Krysta in some obscure way. He wondered if he'd been obsessed with her for months but had been too exhausted to realize it. Now, after a good night's sleep, he was crazy with longing.

Finally he settled on walking the streets, although even that didn't help much. It was Valentine's Day, and everywhere he looked, he saw lovers—a couple hunched over an intimate table in a restaurant, another strolling with their arms around each other, still another kissing on a street corner while they waited for the light to change. It was the most romantic of days, and he was in the most romantic of moods, but Krysta wasn't here.

Eventually he picked up his contacts late in the afternoon and headed back to the hotel to wait for Krysta. Once inside the room he slapped his forehead as he remembered that she was supposed to be on a local talk show and he'd planned to watch. It was already five minutes past the time the segment was scheduled to air.

He grabbed the remote and turned on the set. Fortunately, he remembered the channel without having to search out the note he'd written to himself, and he pushed the buttons to tune it in. Sure enough, there was Krysta in her short little skirt and saucy little smile. Krysta and a female talk-show host were seated in front of a large red cardboard heart fringed in white lace.

"And although you admit your pseudonym is part of a marketing plan, it's obvious you don't intend to reveal your *real* name on this show."

"I don't consider it important at this point," Krysta said.

Good girl, Jack thought.

"So we'll drop that line of inquiry and move on to

something we can talk about, your prize-winning book," the interviewer said. "Manchester supplied me with a few excerpts from *Uptown Girl* so I'd be acquainted with your style. You're a very sensual writer, Candy."

"Effective writing concentrates on the senses," Krysta said.

Nice line, Jack thought. He didn't remember telling her that one.

"I'm particularly impressed with your love scenes," the interviewer continued. "Where do you get your ideas?" she added, looking as if she'd come up with the most stunningly original question in the universe.

"I observe, and I've developed my powers of imagination," Krysta replied earnestly, as if the question had been a brilliant one.

"Beautiful," Jack muttered, admiring the hell out the way she gazed with calm confidence at her interviewer, as if she'd been on television for years.

"Women writers seem to have a particular gift for the nuances between a couple making love," the interviewer said. "Would you agree?"

"Absolutely not. Men are perfectly capable of writing sensitively about lovemaking."

Jack silently thanked her.

"They may be capable of it, but more often than not a male writer will give you a wham, bam, thank-you-ma'am type of scene."

"That may be true for some writers," Krysta said, "but it's still unfair to make generalizations that a man can't write about love."

The interviewer laughed. "Name someone."

"Jack Killigan."

Jack nearly fell off the couch.

"I've never heard of him," the interviewer said.

"Don't worry, you will."

"What has he published?"

Jack clenched his teeth together. She was going to spill the beans right on television. He couldn't believe it.

"He hasn't published anything yet," Krysta said, "but I'm certain he will someday. And he writes beautiful love scenes."

The breath whooshed out of Jack's lungs. That was close. Too close. She was improvising again, and he didn't like it.

"Sounds like the perfect Valentine guy to me," the interviewer said.

Jack leaned forward. Was it makeup, or was Krysta blushing?

"He is," she said.

Jack's heart beat faster.

"Well, we're out of time, folks," the interviewer said. "We've spent the past ten minutes with Candy Valentine, who made the most of this romantic season by winning Manchester Publishing's Valentine's Day contest for unpublished writers. Her sexy romance, titled *Uptown Girl* will be out in time for Valentine's Day next year, right, Candy?"

"That's right."

"And I can hardly wait. Folks, this is one hot read."

The station shifted to a commercial, and that was the end of Krysta's appearance on the show. Jack flicked off the set and thought about what he'd just heard.

Krysta had said he wrote good love scenes, but that was old news. The interviewer, not Krysta, had been the one who'd called him "the perfect Valentine guy," and Krysta had merely agreed with him. She could hardly have done anything else under the circumstances. It probably meant nothing, nothing at all. Unless she really *had* been blushing when she said it. Then it could mean that he'd just gained the whole world.

CONVINCING STEPHANIE that she needed to spend the night alone and order up room service had been difficult, but Krysta had finally managed it. The truth had worked—she was dead on her feet after two days of being a celebrity. Her tote bag over one arm and the huge heart-shaped box of candy she'd received from Manchester under the other, she fumbled as she tried to put her card key in the lock. The door opened, anyway.

She looked into the warm welcome of Jack's eyes and her heart turned over. "Hi."

"Hi. You look exhausted." He drew her inside.

He looked so damn good to her. For some reason he wasn't wearing his glasses, and with his newly styled hair, a recent shave and a decent night's sleep, he was quite a revelation. "To be honest, I am exhausted."

"You can be perfectly honest with me." He took her bag and box of candy and set them on the coffee table before helping her off with her coat.

"That's good to hear." As he took her coat she caught a whiff of his after-shave, and some of her exhaustion faded. "I've been tossing lies around all day. Maybe that's why I'm so tired." She stepped out of her heels and wiggled her toes in the carpet.

"How about a warm bath and some dinner?"

It sounded like a wonderful start. She nodded.

"I'll get the bath water running if you'll put in the dinner order."

She gazed at him and wondered how she'd missed noticing when they were growing up together that he was so handsome, so sexy. "Better put on your glasses so you can tell the hot tap from the cold."

He grinned. "Don't worry. I'll manage."

After he left the room she shrugged and picked up the menu. If he wanted to stumble around without his glasses, it wasn't really her concern. One thing was for sure, his magnetic gaze was even more powerful without that barrier of glass. The more she stared into those blue eyes, the more she longed to forget about Derek, forget about Jack's uncertain future, forget about her own financial burdens, and live out a fantasy in this hotel room with Jack.

She ordered the largest steak on the menu with the usual trimmings of baked potato, sour cream, butter and a dinner salad. She added a bottle of cabernet, a pot of coffee and a piece of chocolate cake. It wasn't her usual fare, but she wasn't in one of her usual moods. The room service operator warned her that the meal would take longer than usual to arrive because it was, after all, Valentine's night.

More time to soak, Krysta thought. Replacing the receiver, she started taking off her suit jacket as she headed for the bedroom.

The rumble of water pounding into the tub and soft music from the bedside radio greeted her as she came through the door. She sighed and went to the closet to hang up her jacket. Glancing at the bedside table, she noticed the plastic heart was still where she'd left it the night before. *Be My Valentine*. Perhaps tonight she'd find out exactly what Jack had meant. A shiver of anticipation ran through her.

The sound of running water stopped and Jack emerged from the bathroom. "I added some of your lavender bath oil to the water," he said.

"Thanks. That sounds—" She paused. "How could you tell what kind it was without your glasses?"

He leaned in the doorway and crossed his arms. "Opened the bottle and sniffed."

"Oh."

He pushed away from the doorjamb. "Better get in there while it's still hot."

"Thanks, Jack. By the way, dinner is going to take a while."

"I'm in no hurry."

"Good." The words fell about her like rose petals. *In no hurry.* Perhaps that was the most seductive quality this man possessed. All her life she'd felt the pressure of time. Here in New York had been even worse. But Jack was the sort of guy who took a relaxed approach to life. And right now, that appealed to Krysta very, very much.

"I'll call you if dinner arrives," he said.

"You're welcome to start listening to the tapes if you want."

"Maybe I will." He started out the door. "By the way, you were great on TV this afternoon." Then he closed the door after him.

So he had seen the show. Had he noticed how flushed she'd become when the interviewer had mentioned that Jack sounded like the perfect Valentine guy? If he had any clue as to how she was beginning to fantasize about making love to him, he hadn't let on.

And although she'd seen some flashes of physical desire in his eyes when he looked at her, he might not want to start a relationship right now when he was on the threshold of a brand-new venture. If Krysta were in his shoes, that's how she'd think.

She took off her makeup, undressed and sank gratefully into the steamy water. Jack had known the perfect temperature to make it, which wasn't surprising considering his sensuous nature. And he'd added just the right bath oil to relax her. As she leaned her head against the rolled-up towel Jack had placed at the end of the tub, Krysta couldn't keep her thoughts away from the man in the other room.

He had a smart mouth, but she was starting to realize that was a coverup for his sensitivity. His ability to write so accurately about human emotions revealed his true makeup, which was warm, caring and very sexy. That glimpse into his psyche was certainly playing havoc with *her* emotions. She'd never been so turned on by a man in her life. Everything about him indicated he'd be a wonderful lover. And her curiosity was killing her.

9

LISTENING TO THE TAPES served both to distract Jack from the beauty bathing in the next room and to humble him about the greatness of his writing. Apparently Krysta's looks had contributed as much to the Candy Valentine project as his book had.

If *Uptown Girl* really took off, he'd need to do something special for Krysta. That might be difficult because nobody was supposed to know of her involvement, and by the time royalties came in her situation might have changed drastically. She could even be married to Derek Hamilton, purveyor of crummy kisses. Now, there was a depressing thought.

Fortunately Krysta had been selective about what she'd recorded, so by the time she emerged from the bedroom wearing a white terry robe, he'd made it through most of the first day.

He shut off the recorder and glanced up. "Feeling better?"

"Much."

She looked like a present ready to be unwrapped, and he wondered if he'd be able to keep his hands to himself. A knock on the door signaled the arrival of room service. Good. Another distraction. Maybe over dinner he'd be able to assess her mood and decide what to do. It had been a long time since he'd attempted a seduction, and he didn't want to miscalculate.

"Better go hide," Krysta said.

"Yeah." He retreated to the moist, fragrant atmosphere of the bedroom and saw that she'd tossed her discarded underwear on the bed, including lacy panties, bra and stockings. Not panty hose, but stockings. He looked around for a garter belt and found none. Both the writer in him and the man wondered how she kept the stockings from falling down, so he picked one up and discovered the lace-decorated top was elasticized.

Rubbing the silky material between his fingers, he imagined her putting the stocking on. He saw her easing it over those pink toenails and guiding the material past her instep. He envisioned the nylon caressing her graceful calf and slender knee before smoothly encasing her thigh in a gentle hug. He laid the stocking back on the bed, closed his eyes and took a deep breath. Sometimes imagination was a curse instead of a blessing. He was thoroughly aroused, but the next step in the evening plan was dinner, not bed.

Behind him, Krysta opened the bedroom door. "Dinner's served."

He was in no shape to walk out that door. "Be right there. I'm going to wash up," he said, and headed for the bathroom. Turning on the faucet, he leaned both hands on the counter and stared at himself in the mirror. "Killigan, you are in danger of making a colossal fool of yourself tonight," he told the frustrated guy reflected back at him. "Take it easy, okay?"

Moments later he had himself under control enough

to return to the living room—a room, it turned out, lit only by candles on the banquet table. He blinked.

"The, um, room service guy did this." Krysta stepped from the shadows. "I guess he'd been given the word from Manchester that Candy Valentine should have a romantic dinner tonight even if she chose to spend it alone."

Jack stood transfixed by his first view of Krysta by candlelight. Exquisite.

"You may not be able to see very well, especially if you'd rather not wear your glasses," she said uncertainly. "We can blow them out and turn the lights back on if this is too much atmosphere for you."

He snapped out of his trance. "No, this is great." He walked over to the table. "I just hope they're not planning to send up somebody from an escort service to make your evening complete."

Her eyes widened. "You don't think they would, do you?"

"I was kidding. I can't imagine anyone taking that kind of liberty if you made it clear that you wanted to be alone."

"Well, I did." She looked at him, but when he returned her gaze she seemed to lose her nerve and glanced away. "I knew we needed to listen to those tapes together, especially the one from the revision session this morning. Maybe we should hear that now."

"Since we don't have a strolling violinist, we might as well." For a moment there, in the candlelight, he'd imagined she might be thinking along the same lines that he had been, but then she'd steered them right back to business.

"I'll find the place on the tape."

He glanced at the table and noticed an open bottle of red wine. While she fooled with the recorder he walked over and lifted the lid covering the plate of food to find out what she'd ordered to go with it. "Steak and baked potato?" he exclaimed in surprise. "Has life in the Big Apple corrupted Krysta Lueckenhoff?"

She laughed. "No, you have."

How he wished that were true. "With one steak knife to our name I guess somebody better start cutting up this roast beast."

"Be my guest." She came over with the tape recorder and snapped it on as she sat across from him. "I think this is the part I wanted you to hear."

As he listened to Stephanie Briggs begin discussing changes she'd like to see in *Uptown Girl*, he cut meat and put it on a saucer for himself before giving Krysta the plate. She took the potato off and plopped it on his saucer, along with some bits of salad. He was listening too intently to question her divvying up of the food.

He ate without giving it much thought while he concentrated on the tape. Thank God Stephanie's suggestions for the book were reasonable and wouldn't require a lot of work, he thought. More than that, they didn't veer much from his original image of the characters.

Then the recorder picked up Krysta's response. *I disagree with your first suggestion,* she said with sickening clarity.

Jack dropped his fork and stared at his dinner companion.

Christine needs to be very angry in that scene with her father, Krysta's taped voice continued. *And I don't think she should cry. That's a wimpy thing for her to do at that point, and she's too strong to break down in front of him.*

Jack hit the stop button on the recorder. "You *argued* with her?"

"Why not?" She seemed totally unrepentant. "Stephanie was wrong."

"But she's the *editor*."

"And I'm a *reader*. I've been buying romances for years, and I know what readers want."

"That may be true, but a first-time author doesn't argue with the editor. Especially not on her very first *point*."

Krysta shoved his hand aside and pressed the play button. "Listen to the rest, Jack."

"You mean the part where she cancels the contract because she realizes I'm going to be too difficult to work with? Krysta, you—"

"Just listen! She went along with it!"

And so she had. Jack gazed across the table at Krysta's smug little smile as Stephanie retracted her original criticism and agreed with Krysta's evaluation of the scene. He stopped the tape again. "Okay, so you got away with it. I sure as hell hope that was the only time you tried that."

"As a matter of fact, she changed three of her five points."

"My God."

"Jack, what's the matter with you? Don't you believe in the integrity of your work?"

"Not as much as you, apparently."

"Then it's a very good thing I handled the revision discussion. Ready to hear the rest of the tape?"

"I don't know if my heart can take it. You're a dangerous woman."

"And one you need, obviously." She punched the play button again.

"If you only knew," Jack murmured.

"What did you say?"

"Nothing."

"Stop your muttering and relax. Someday you'll thank me for being so assertive on your behalf."

He found relaxing almost impossible as Krysta and Stephanie chose to discuss a love scene next.

I'll bow to your judgment on this, Candy, Stephanie said. *But I wonder if Jake shouldn't be a little more frenzied as he makes love to Christine that first time. After all, he wants her very much.*

That's the beauty of his restrained approach, Krysta replied. *I can guarantee that women will go crazy imagining themselves being seduced so slowly and expertly. His controlled passion makes him even more exciting.*

Jack risked a glance at Krysta and caught her looking at him. Was that a gleam of desire in her eyes, or the candlelight playing tricks on him? He'd give anything to know if this conversation was doing the same thing to her that it was doing to him. She glanced away, and he could swear she was blushing. He barely heard the rest of the tape and hardly tasted the food on his plate.

When the discussion moved to the TV interview that afternoon, Krysta turned off the tape. "What do you think?"

I think I'll go crazy if I don't make love to you very soon. "I think you're amazing," he said. It was all he had courage for. "You did a great job with Stephanie."

"Thank you."

He sipped his wine and watched the candlelight caress her soft skin and lustrous hair. "That haircut really does suit you. I would have voted against cutting it, but now I see I would have been wrong."

Her eyes grew luminous. "I'm glad you like it."

Perhaps it was only the candlelight that put that welcoming light in her eyes. Maybe it was only the force of his own desire that made her look like a woman who wanted to be loved. He decided to bring up the television show. After all, she'd said publicly that he wrote great love scenes. "You mentioned something in your interview today that I—"

"Oh, I almost forgot! I have the proofs from the photo session, if you'd like to see them."

"Okay." Well, he probably had his answer. She wanted to stick with business matters. Taking the wine bottle and his water glass, he left the table. "Bring your glass, and we'll sit on the couch and go through them." He was glad he hadn't asked about the television show. He might not have liked what he heard.

"You'd better get your glasses for this," she said. "I'm supposed to give Stephanie my favorites tomorrow, and I want your input considering that one of these will end up on the dust jacket."

"I don't need my glasses." He snapped on a lamp next to the couch.

She blew out the candles and walked toward the couch, her wine goblet in her hand. "Look, I know they must bother you, with that tape on them, but I want you to be able to see these pictures, Jack. You can take the glasses off again when we're finished."

He sat on the couch and crossed his ankle over his

knee before taking a sip of his wine. "I'm wearing contact lenses."

Her mouth dropped open. "I don't believe you." Still holding her goblet she sat beside him and peered into his eyes. "You *are*. When did this happen?"

"I picked them up today." Only a few inches and his lips would be on hers. His heart beat faster. But she wasn't offering to kiss him. She was only examining his new lenses. Yet her breathing seemed a little quicker, a little more shallow.

She moved back a bit and studied him. "You arranged for contact lenses in that short a time? You must have paid a fortune. The haircut was one thing, but buying contacts in a strange city on short notice is really beyond understanding." The words sounded like Krysta, but her soft tone caught his attention.

"I didn't pay for them. I—"

"Oh, Jack. Don't tell me you put them on credit. That's even more ridiculous than—"

He pressed a finger against her lips. It was a subtle move, one that could go nowhere, or start them on a long, sweet journey. He'd know by her reaction to his touch which it would be. "Hey," he said gently. "Stop talking for five seconds and let me tell you how I got the haircut and the contact lenses."

Her eyes darkened a fraction.

A less observant man might have missed the change, but Jack had written about such moments, and he didn't miss it. Slowly he removed his finger, but he kept eye contact. He wanted to build on what he'd started. Briefly he told her about tackling the mugger, trashing his glasses and accepting the offer of the grateful businessman to pay for contact lenses and a haircut.

"You could have been killed," she murmured, her gaze never leaving his, her fingers tight around the stem of her glass. "You should never have tried to stop him."

"I acted on instinct. There was no conscious decision on my part."

"Now, that really scares me, thinking you might do something foolish like that again."

"Why?" he asked quietly.

She swallowed. "Because I care what happens to you."

"You mean whether I take my vitamins or get enough sleep? That sort of thing?" He heard the edge of frustration in his voice but couldn't control it.

"Well, that, and whether you're happy...and...and if you'll find someone special some day."

"You're worried about my love life?"

"Not worried so much as..." She closed her eyes and took a long, shaky breath. "I can't stand it another minute."

He noticed the tremor that passed through her, and hoped he could guess what she was about to say. "Can't stand what?" His heart thudded wildly.

"Wondering." Slowly she opened her eyes, and they flashed green fire. "Can you kiss the way you wrote about it in the book?"

The blood roared in his ears. "Yes."

"Would you...show me?"

He turned away to set his glass on the coffee table. Then he took her goblet from her unresisting fingers and put it beside his before turning back to her. His hands shook slightly as he cupped her face with both hands, but the sensation of her warm skin beneath his fingers steadied him. He wanted nothing more than to kiss her the way she was meant to be kissed. If this was all he was ever allowed, it would have to be enough. And he would make sure that she never forgot the next few minutes for as long as she lived.

"Close your eyes," he murmured, gazing down at her. "Close your eyes, and empty your mind of everything else but this."

She looked more hesitant and vulnerable than he'd ever seen her. "I don't know if I can, Jack."

"You can."

"Should I...hold you?"

"No. I'll hold you." *For as along as you'll allow it.*

With a little sigh she allowed her eyes to drift closed.

"Happy Valentine's Day," he whispered. He started with her temples, brushing them with his lips before pressing his mouth against the gently beating pulse there. He breathed in the fragrance of her hair as he slid his fingers into the thick mass of curls.

Holding her with firm pressure, he tilted her head back and kissed her closed eyes, willing her to see only pleasure, feel only delight. He stroked his fingers through her hair to cup the back of her head, then guided her backward until her head rested in his hands and her throat lay exposed.

Beginning at the tender hollow that throbbed with excitement, he settled his mouth there, heating her already warm skin as he moved up the column of her throat with languid kisses. Her breathing quickened with each feathery touch. And each time his lips brushed her petal-soft skin, his soul became more enmeshed in the pure joy of loving her at last.

He drew out the moment, drew out the risk for both

of them. Searching out the sensitive spot behind the lobe of her ear, he rejoiced in her tiny gasp of surprise as he caressed her there. He traced the line of her jaw in reverent detail, and as his path took him closer to the corner of her mouth, she began to quiver beneath him.

He teased her with a soft touch at one corner, a gentle kiss at the other. Her lips parted on a slight moan. He angled his mouth above hers, allowing her to sense him there, to feel his breath and to know he drew nearer. He touched down with the lightness of a breeze, the warmth of a sunbeam, and the gentle insistence of a man in love.

It was his secret weapon, the force that made a mockery of mere technique. He loved her, had loved her for months, perhaps for years. Slowly he took command of her mouth and tried to tell her. The message was gentle at first, as he molded his lips to hers and savored the velvet softness and the delicate taste of her. He paid homage as a supplicant might.

Until the fever took her.

With a groan of surrender she pulled him in deeper, and as supplication transformed to demand, and sweetness to desperate hunger, he lifted his mouth from hers and drew back, although his whole being rebelled at being denied the satisfaction of loving her completely and thoroughly. But that next step would not be taken mindlessly. Too much depended on what happened next to let themselves fall into bed without thinking. He'd asked her to empty her mind. Now he would ask her to think.

She didn't open her eyes at first, and it was all he could do not to return to those provocatively parted lips.

Then gradually her eyelids lifted to reveal a gaze that would melt steel. Her voice was blurred with passion. "Why did you stop?"

His breathing was none too steady. "Because it was the end of the kiss."

"I don't think so."

"You asked for a kiss. That's what you got."

Awareness dawned in her expression. "I'm supposed to ask if I want...more?"

"Yes."

Her voice was husky with passion. "And why is that?"

"Because I'm not the vice president of a company and probably won't ever be one. Because I understand perfectly why you want financial stability in a man, and I may never have that. Because I'm in no position to make promises. If I were a stronger man, I'd tell you to stay the hell away from me. I don't fit into your game plan."

A sultry smile tipped the corners of her well-kissed mouth. "Are you finished?"

"Yes."

"I liked the kiss, Jack." Her slow, easy speech was the exact opposite of the brisk way she usually talked. "I liked it a lot."

Apparently he'd transformed her into a seductress, he thought in wonder as he gazed at her and waited for the rest.

"And I was wondering..."

He lifted his eyebrows as she paused dramatically.

"I was wondering if you can make love the way you wrote in your book."

He thought his lungs would explode. "Yes," he said, and scooped her up off the couch.

As he carried her into the bedroom, the tie on her robe slipped and the garment fell open. He glanced down at the daisy nightie she wore underneath, then back into her face. "Did you plan for this to happen all along?"

"No." She smiled up at him. "But I thought if it did, you might want to do a little research on exactly how the nightie comes off."

"What you read that day's been destroyed."

"Jack! It was good!"

Pushing her discarded underwear aside, he eased her down to the bed and smoothed the hair away from her face. "This will be, too. And some things aren't meant to be in print."

10

KRYSTA TREMBLED in anticipation as she gazed up into Jack's face and realized that soon she would know what it was like to be loved by him. She thought of the scene in *Uptown Girl* when Jake had first made love to Christine. Jake and Christine. Jack and Krysta. She hadn't noticed before.

She touched his cheek. "The characters in your book—"

"Are not us."

"But the names. They're almost like ours."

"Almost." He trailed a finger across her lips. "I made those characters just enough like us to inspire me. But Christine's not you, because I hadn't ever... I didn't know you well enough."

Her mouth tingled where he'd touched her. "We hadn't ever made love."

"Only in my mind."

The idea that he'd imagined making love to her while he wrote took her breath away. "So Jake isn't you, either?"

"No."

"He's...a pretty sexy guy."

The corners of his mouth twitched as if he was holding back a smile. "Are you saying I'm in competition with somebody I made up?"

"Well..."

"Forget Jake. He's not real." He leaned down, his lips close to hers. "But I am," he murmured just before he carried her away with another mind-shattering kiss.

She tangled her fingers in his hair and invited him to deepen the embrace. When at last she felt the thrust of his tongue, desire shook her with a force that made her gasp. He'd done nothing more than kiss her and she was already molten and ready for him, already fumbling with the buttons of his shirt. He caught her hands and finished the job far more efficiently than she ever could have. She ran her hands over the firm muscles of his chest and felt the answering shudder beneath her palms.

Lifting his mouth from hers, he gazed down at her with an intensity that tightened the coil of excitement deep inside another delicious notch. Moving from the bed, he finished undressing, his attention remaining focused on her the entire time. She remembered this part of his fictional love scene, remembered how Christine had responded to the first sight of her lover's body. In the soft light from the bedside lamp, Krysta feasted on the unveiling of Jack, thoroughly aroused, and very real. In that moment she abandoned all thought of fictional heroes.

He stooped to the floor and pulled some small cellophane packages out of his pocket before laying them on the bedside table.

So there was some premeditation involved, she thought. The idea excited her even more. "Do optometrists give out those little packages with new sets of contact lenses?" she murmured. "I suppose it makes sense. If you're sexier, you'll probably have reason to use—"

"You know what?" He levered his body to the bed.

The stimulation of having an unclothed Jack right there beside her made speaking almost impossible. She longed to touch him but was finding herself more than a little shy about where to begin. "No, what?"

"I'm amazed you didn't ask me about condoms before we ever came in here. I thought we'd have to discuss which brand to use."

It was a legitimate concern, but for some reason her brain didn't seem to be functioning very well right now. She cleared her throat. "Now that you mention it, wh—"

"Too late," he said, sliding off the sleeves of her bathrobe. "We're not going to discuss it now. It's a good brand."

"But—"

"Be quiet, Krysta." His smile was gentle. "For once in your life, relax and let somebody else take charge."

It was the sort of command she'd waited a lifetime to hear. And take charge he did. So this was what it was like to tremble in anticipation of a man's touch. She'd never known. But she'd never known a lover with instincts like Jack's, a lover who spurned the obvious and embraced the subtle, a lover who specialized in the art of surprise.

He stretched her arm out and stroked her fingers as if they were the most erogenous part of her. And for the moment, they were. Then he moved to her palm, and the inside of her wrist, igniting bonfires along his path.

As he brushed his fingers along the underside of her arm, she imagined that same touch on her inner thigh and moaned in anticipation. "Kiss me, Jack," she begged.

"I thought you were going to let me be in charge," he murmured.

Her breathing grew shallow as he continued his ministrations to her other arm. "Not even any...requests?" she asked.

"I'll consider them."

She let out her breath on a long sigh. "Then kiss me, Jack."

He did, sliding down the bed to place his lips against the arch of her foot. As he ran his tongue into the crevices between her toes, she began to throb with the intensity of wanting him. She trembled as he kissed his way with careful intent up her calf and behind her knee. When his lips caressed her inner thigh, she thought she might go out of her mind.

And still he hadn't removed her nightie. She was ready to tear the material off herself, but he'd clasped both her hands in his, intertwining their fingers as he approached the moist center so ready for him. And then he moved past that pulsing spot without touching her there and came back to her side again. She was wild to have him.

Releasing her hands, he drew the nightie over her head. Except for the slight trembling of his hand as he cupped her breast, he seemed to be in perfect control. She arched into his caress, desperate for his mouth to relieve the aching need swelling in her breasts.

She'd expected him to go slowly here, too, but it was as if he knew the moment for light caresses had ended. He took her breast into his mouth fully and deliberately, giving her such pleasure that tears filled her eyes.

The pace accelerated. His touch was more demanding than gentle as he slid his hand down to her waist. When he moved astride her, she thought he might sheathe himself and take her then and there. And, oh, she wanted that. The pressure had become so intense that all she could think of was having him fill her and end the sweet torture he'd begun.

But he didn't reach for the package on the bedside table. Instead, he trailed kisses down the valley between her ribs as he slid both hands beneath her bottom. Before she realized his intent, he'd lifted her to his waiting mouth for a caress that splintered all semblance of self-control. She could no more stop the cataclysmic response he brought forth than stop breathing. She cried out as wave upon wave took her with a force that left her gasping and limp in the cradle of his strong hands.

At last he lowered her gently to the bed and returned to her side. He smoothed the tangled hair from her cheeks as he covered her face with kisses. She had no breath, no words to tell him how he'd made her feel, but he seemed to know.

She felt dazed and disoriented as she looked into his eyes. "But I still want—"

"Good." He lingered a moment and brushed his mouth against hers. "So do I."

The taste of passion on his lips began the spiral of need all over again. "Now, Jack," she urged. "I want you."

He outlined her mouth with the tip of his tongue. "That sounds like an order."

She groaned in frustration.

With a soft chuckle he reached over to the bedside table for the condom. The soft snap of the latex as it covered his erection sent a hot new surge of longing through her.

"Come here," he whispered, slipping his arm beneath her and lifting her gently. She hadn't expected this would be what he'd want now, but she followed his guidance and positioned herself above him.

"Why this way?" she murmured.

His voice was ragged with need. "Because you need to be in control again."

She hesitated. Was there censure in his tone or was it merely roughened with desire? "Jack, I—"

"It's okay, Krysta. I'm man enough to let you lead."

"I believe you are." She gazed into his eyes as she slowly lowered herself, taking him deeper and deeper inside her. She'd never seen a blue so intense as the color of his eyes as she accepted him completely inside her.

He understood so much, including her need to give to him as he'd given to her. Bracing her hands on either side of his shoulders, she initiated a slow rhythm and watched his eyes darken. Knowing that she was bestowing pleasure built the tension in her once again, and although she concentrated on him, her own needs began to clamor for satisfaction.

But she wanted him to know that he'd already taught her something about making love. She pushed aside her own desires and tuned in to the sound of his breathing, allowing that to guide her into an ever-accelerating motion. She watched his eyes and listened to the soft groans of pleasure as his hips moved in concert with hers. And for a brief time she felt what he felt and knew just when to increase the pressure, when to ease away, and when, at last, to take him on a glorious ride over the brink. To her complete surprise, she careened over the edge with him, as if they'd truly become one mind, one heart, one soul.

As the pieces of her world slowly realigned themselves again, she sank to his chest and laid her cheek over his beating heart. She'd had no idea. Nothing, not even Jack's own words on paper, had prepared her for such cataclysmic lovemaking. She thought of trying to tell him all that was in her heart, but decided she could never do justice to what she felt. Jack was the wordsmith, not her, and besides, he was so sensitive to her feelings he must know what he'd accomplished.

She closed her eyes and snuggled against him. He reached a hand to stroke her hair. For the first time in her life she felt completely, utterly at peace.

SHE WAS OBVIOUSLY planning to keep her reaction to herself, Jack thought with some impatience. They lay propped against the headboard, pillows behind them, and they'd turned on the other bedside lamp so they'd have plenty of light to study the photos for the dust jacket.

Jack wasn't quite sure how to interpret Krysta's silence about their lovemaking. She'd never been slow to offer her opinion of his behavior before. After they'd made love she'd lain quietly with him for several long minutes. He'd needed some recovery time, himself, so he hadn't been ready for an immediate critique. But he'd expected her to eventually make some comment about what they'd just shared.

He'd be damned if he'd ask her for one, though. That old "Was it good for you?" routine wasn't his style. He knew it had been good for her, and it had been spectacular for him. But he'd had the decided impression that he was on trial, and he'd sure like to hear the results.

That didn't seem likely. Whatever Krysta thought about his lovemaking, she wasn't talking. So he relaxed here in bed with her, hip to naked hip like newlyweds, the box of valentine candy open with brown candy wrappers scattered over the covers, and Candy Valentine's publicity photos spread before them. Krysta had suggested getting them out, which was when he'd begun to suspect she wasn't going to discuss her reaction to the obvious pleasure he'd given her.

So maybe they wouldn't talk about it. Maybe they'd just do it some more. He didn't think she'd have a problem with that. Perhaps he expected too much in the way of verbal reassurance. Not everyone was into words the way he was. Hell, almost nobody was.

If he'd been writing this scene he would give Krysta dialogue telling him that he was the best lover she'd ever had. Unfortunately he wasn't writing this scene. All along he'd been teasing her about wanting to be in control. Maybe it was time to admit his own need for control, which he exercised every time he wrote a book, and which he longed to exercise in real life, truth be told.

"I think this is my favorite." Krysta held up a five-by-seven proof of her sitting sideways on a stool in the leather suit, her legs crossed, her upper body turned toward the camera, and a decidedly come-hither look on her face.

Jack felt a twinge of jealousy. "How did he get you to look at him like that?"

"Did I say it was a male photographer?"

"No, but I'll bet it was."

"And you'd be right." She shifted slightly, which rubbed her silky thigh against him. "He told me to think of the sexiest guy I knew."

"Is that so?" He glanced at her.

Reaching down to pick a chocolate out of the box, she kept looking through the photos without seeming to notice that he was staring at her. "This one's not bad, either." She held up one in which she was leaning against a post while wearing a full-length white coat with a white fur collar that brushed her cheeks. She was holding the heart-shaped box of candy she'd brought home tonight. Narrowing her eyes at the picture, she took a bite of the chocolate, exposing a creamy center. "Classier, I think. Which one do you—"

"And who might that be?" Jack asked, not giving a damn about the pictures when they had more important matters to discuss.

"Who might who be?" She took another dainty bite of the candy.

"You know good and well. The sexiest guy you know." He took the proofs away from her.

"Hey!" She reached for the proofs. "We need to go over those."

"Later." He held them out of reach.

"Jack." She made another grab.

He dumped them on the floor, then took her by the shoulders and toppled her backward across the mattress. "Who's the sexiest guy you know?"

She laughed and squirmed beneath him. "Mel Gibson."

"Oh, yeah? On what grounds?"

"You obviously didn't see *Braveheart* or you wouldn't ask." She grinned up at him and popped the last of the candy in her mouth.

"I can see we still have a little trouble sorting out the difference between fantasy and reality around here." He shifted his weight so he had better access to her inviting body. "The sexiest guy you know isn't Mel Gibson."

"Yes, it is."

Putting a firm hand between her thighs, he kissed her smiling lips and tasted chocolate. Then he lifted his head as he stroked upward and probed deep. "You don't know Mel Gibson," he murmured. "All you know is the fantasy he creates."

She drew in her breath. "I suppose you're some sort of authority."

"I suppose I am. I'm in the fantasy business, myself." He'd aroused her in seconds. He could send her spiraling into orgasm in seconds more. That gave him some satisfaction, at least. "Who were you thinking of when the photographer took that picture?"

"I..." She shifted the candy in her mouth. "I can't think of anything when you...do that."

He leaned down. "You'd better give me that piece of chocolate before you choke on it," he whispered.

"No."

"Yes." He delved into her mouth with his tongue and captured the bit of candy.

"I want that," she murmured.

"But you want this more." The chocolate was sweet

on his tongue as he massaged the tight little bud that gave her such pleasure.

Her fingernails dug into his shoulders as she drew closer to the abyss. "Jack..."

"So you thought of me when he took the picture?" Ah, she was nearly there.

"I...yes!" She arched upward.

"Thank you, Krysta." He settled his mouth over hers and drank in her gasps as he pushed his fingers in deep to absorb her contractions.

Afterward, she lay so quietly beneath him that he thought she might have drifted off to sleep. And he vowed not to wake her, even though he was hard and wanting her again.

Then her hand curled around his erection, and all his senses went on alert.

"You've wrung that confession out of me by devious means," she said, her voice silky as the stockings she'd worn that day. "And now I intend to get a confession out of you with the same method."

He'd tell her anything she wanted to know, but that wouldn't be much fun. "Good luck. I'm a past master at keeping my own counsel."

Her hand glided upward, then back down. "I want to know when you bought those condoms."

He sucked in a breath as she repeated her motion and lingered over the sensitive tip. "What difference does it make?" he asked.

"I want to know how long you've been planning this evening's entertainment." She wriggled from beneath him and continued her caress. She seemed to understand more about male anatomy than he'd given her credit for. "I want to know if this was part of the plan all along."

"I don't see that it..." He couldn't finish the sentence. In one graceful movement she arranged things so that she could take him in her mouth. "Matters," he finished, groaning.

After driving him very nearly crazy, she lifted her head to give him an angelic smile. "Oh, it matters." Her thumb had found his trigger point and she was using her knowledge to great advantage.

He clenched his jaw and closed his eyes as he fought to stay in control. It was a mistake. He opened his eyes when he heard the rip of cellophane. She'd used her teeth and one free hand to open the package, and now she was rolling a condom over his throbbing penis and torturing him every step of the way.

"Want to tell me yet?" she asked.

Not yet, answered his highly stimulated body. But when she was finished, he grabbed her shoulders and rolled her to her back.

Her eyes sparkled with fun as she gazed up at him. Her thighs remained clamped together. "Not until you tell me."

He'd never forced a woman in his life and he wasn't about to start now. He let her win. "I bought them when you agreed to come on this trip," he said.

"That long ago?"

"It was a wild dream, not a calculated plot. I was prepared to take every one of them home unused."

She opened her thighs and drew him toward her. "Doesn't look like that will happen."

"No, it doesn't." He claimed her with one quick thrust.

She gasped and her eyes widened in surprise.

"Did you think I'd always go slow and easy?" he murmured.

She cupped his face in her hands. "With you, I never know what to think."

He drew back and pushed in tight again. "That makes two of us." It was the closest he could come to asking her to talk to him.

She gazed at him in wonder. "You don't know how you've affected me?"

"I can only guess."

"I was sure you knew. You've taken me where no one else ever has. I—" She drew a breath. "Compared to you, I feel...inadequate."

"Inadequate?" He looked at her in disbelief. "But you're the most beautiful, most responsive woman I've ever—" He shook his head. "*Inadequate.* That word has no business being in the same room with you, Krysta."

She moved provocatively beneath him. "Love me, Jack. Love me until morning comes."

11

As Krysta yawned and stretched the next morning, her toe hit something that clattered to the floor. She leaned over the edge of the bed to discover the heart-shaped box of candy upended and chocolates everywhere. Then she glanced at her travel alarm on the bedside table. The travel alarm she hadn't set the night before.

"Oh, my God!" She leaped out of bed and stepped on a caramel cream and a chocolate nougat. "Dammit! Oh, yuck!"

"I gather you're not a morning person," Jack said, lifting his head off the pillow.

She hardly spared him a glance as she tottered on one foot and lifted the other while trying to scrape the chocolate from her sole. She lost her balance and staggered, only to step on a dark chocolate with a cherry center. "I hate candy!" she moaned.

"The food or the author?"

"Both, at the moment." She walked stiff-legged on her heels into the bathroom. "I have to be ready in fifteen minutes, Jack," she called over her shoulder.

"If memory serves, I can manage it in less time than that."

"Will you stop with the one-liners?" She held on to the door frame for balance and poked her head around it to glare at him. Her irritation evaporated at the sight of Jack lying there propped on one elbow, the sheet pulled up only as far as his waist, his hair deliciously tousled, and a seductive grin on his beard-stubbled face. She was falling in love with him. That might not be the prudent thing to do under her current financial circumstances, but the truth was inescapable. Jack was the man she'd dreamed of all her life.

"I'll be glad to take care of that chocolate for you," he said softly.

She was quite sure he would, and she'd love to let him. He might even smear more chocolate around just to give him an excuse to do something sinfully sensuous.

Not that Jack needed an excuse. He was a sexy rogue, no doubt about it, but somebody had to think of the business side of things this morning. That somebody would obviously have to be her. She'd taken on the responsibility, and she was determined to do the best job she possibly could of being his alter-ego.

"The limo will arrive in fourteen minutes to take me to have breakfast with Stephanie," she said. "Candy Valentine has established herself as a punctual person. I need your help."

"That's the trouble with reputations." He shifted his weight, causing his shoulder muscles to bunch appealingly. "You have to uphold them. I think maybe we should—"

"Jack, this is important. I'm pretty sure Stephanie will make an offer on your next book this morning."

He grew still. "You are?"

"I am."

His gaze narrowed. "And if she does, you're planning to negotiate the contract?"

"Of course."

"I don't like the sound of this."

"I'll be reasonable."

"Like last time when you demanded double the money?"

"You got it, didn't you? Listen, Jack, if I don't get down there in ten minutes, Stephanie will be sipping coffee by herself in the Rose Room of the Algonquin, and no matter how you look at it, that would be a mistake."

He threw back the covers. "Okay. Go take your shower. I'll talk to you while you're in there."

It took all the discipline she possessed to turn her back on his magnificent body and head for the shower. She consoled herself with the fact that she was doing it all for him. "Better pick up the candy first," she cautioned before she twisted the handles of the shower.

"Do you know that the Algonquin is where Dorothy Parker and a lot of other writers from the Roaring Twenties used to hang out?" Jack called over the sound of the spray.

"No," she called back.

"I'd guess that's why Stephanie's taking you there, so you'd better act impressed."

"Got it. Thanks for the tip." She took the shortest shower in history, and Jack was still kneeling on the floor searching for chocolate when she returned to the bedroom with a towel wrapped around her.

He glanced up. "This candy reproduced during the night. There's twice as much here as there was yesterday."

"It was a double-layered box." She stepped carefully as she walked past him toward the closet.

His hand circled her ankle.

She spared him a quick glance. "Jack, I—"

"Good morning."

Once again, she melted before the intensity of his gaze. What she wouldn't give to have set that alarm. "Good morning." The mere touch of his hand on her ankle reawakened her desire, demonstrating how close to the surface her passion for him remained, even after hours of making love. "So I've brought you to your knees," she said, her tone deliberately light.

"Yes."

She swallowed. The banter was gone from his expression, and the resistance nearly gone from her heart.

"Thank you for an incredible night," he said.

"It was incredible, Jack."

His thumb caressed her instep. "When will your breakfast with Stephanie be over?"

"I'm not sure." Heat surged through her. "How about this? No matter what the contract offer is, I'll tell her I want to come back to the hotel and have some time alone to mull it over. That way, you can have input."

A slow grin appeared on his handsome face. "Oh, Krysta, I like the way you phrased that."

She couldn't help laughing, even though it was shameful that he couldn't keep his mind on business at such a critical time. "You are incorrigible."

"It's one of my finer qualities."

"Let me go, Jack. I have to get dressed."

"More's the pity." But he released her ankle and went back to hunting for the chocolates. "Do you think we should eat these?"

"Absolutely not." She whipped through her dressing routine, throwing on underwear and a green linen pantsuit. "You don't know what's been on that floor. Rug-cleaning chemicals for one thing. Throw them away. Make yourself some coffee and I'll smuggle croissants or something back from the Rose Room."

"What about the maid finding me here? I don't want to leave and take a chance on being gone when you come back. Not when I've been promised input."

She tried to send him a reproving glance and failed miserably. "I'll put the Do Not Disturb sign out. She can make up the room later in the day, for once."

"Or not at all."

"Jack, you're a hedonist." She grabbed her coat from the closet.

"An incorrigible hedonist. That makes me pretty close to perfect."

"I'm outta here," she said, hurrying past him.

"Y'all come back," he said softly.

She gave him one last, yearning glance. "I will." He probably thought she was so regimented that it was easy for her to walk out of the room. Little did he know that her own hedonistic tendencies grew stronger every time he looked into her eyes the way he was doing now. "I'll see you soon," she said, and left.

STEPHANIE WAS, IN FACT, sipping coffee when Krysta arrived at the Rose Room a bare four minutes late.

Holding the tote bag containing the tape recorder she'd already turned on, Krysta glanced around. The breakfast crowd at the Algonquin was definitely upscale. She suspected Armani and Gucci were well-represented by the customers who sat on cranberry-upholstered chairs drawn up to white linen-covered tables. Ornate white molding, cranberry-colored walls, crystal chandeliers and gold-plated wall sconces completed the turn-of-the-century elegance.

"So this is where Dorothy and the gang hung out," Krysta said to Stephanie as the waiter pulled out her chair.

"I thought you'd appreciate eating here." Stephanie motioned for the waiter to bring Krysta some coffee. "Did you have a nice Valentine's night, all alone in your suite?"

Krysta grabbed her napkin and ducked her head while she made a big production of putting the napkin in her lap. "Very restful, thanks." She cleared her throat and looked up, hoping that she was revealing nothing in her expression.

"From the pink in your cheeks I'm beginning to wonder if you were up there watching adult movies. Is that how you get inspired?"

Krysta managed to laugh. Adult movies were as good an excuse as any for her reaction, she decided. "You've found me out. I really don't watch them ordinarily, but there I was with titles like *Cheeky Cheerleaders* staring me in the face, and I've always been curious about movies like that."

Stephanie regarded her over the rim of her coffee cup. "And?"

"Pretty repetitious, actually."

Stephanie nodded. "Most of them are produced by men for men, I suspect. If they've tried to appeal to women, they obviously don't know how, which isn't surprising. It's a rare man who understands what arouses a woman."

"Very rare," Krysta agreed. *And I've found one.*

"That's why books like yours sell so well, of course. We love to read about a man like Jake and imagine him making love to us, just as you pointed out in our discussion yesterday."

Imagination pales next to the real thing, Krysta thought.

"I'd be very surprised if a man could ever capture the erotic tone you've created in *Uptown Girl.*"

"Oh, I'm not so sure about that."

"Well, it doesn't much matter if they could or not. You've done a wonderful job, Candy." Stephanie picked up the menu and signaled their waiter. "Let's order, and then we can talk."

Krysta noticed a selection that included croissants and ordered that, thinking that she'd find some way to put the croissants in her tote bag when Stephanie wasn't watching. It wasn't great nutrition, but better than the chocolate chip cookies Jack might filch from the honor bar in the suite.

She let Stephanie direct the conversation, and the editor seemed to be in no hurry to discuss business beyond her initial praise of Candy's work. They covered politics, the climate in the Seattle area, and Stephanie's love of houseplants. Krysta enjoyed the conversation because she found she had much in common with Stephanie, but she was itching to get down to brass tacks. Then she could return to the suite, where she could get down to…a few other things.

In addition to her eagerness to talk about Jack's new book, she hadn't found a good time to slip the croissants into her tote bag. Smuggling food was a lot tougher in this one-on-one situation than it had been during the raucous group dinner at Sardi's.

"I think we need more coffee," Stephanie said and turned to locate their waiter.

Seizing the moment, Krysta grabbed the croissants from the basket beside her plate and dropped them into the tote bag.

Stephanie turned back more quickly than Krysta had expected. She glanced at the bread basket and then at Krysta.

Krysta knew she was blushing, knew she'd been caught. "I—uh—was pretty full, but these looked wonderful. I didn't think this was the sort of restaurant where one asked for a doggie bag."

"Of course you can ask for a doggie bag. In fact, I'll order more croissants and have them wrapped for you. Take those out and we'll add them to the batch."

Krysta wished the tote was big enough for her to crawl into after the croissants and disappear. "That's not necessary, really. Just these two will be fine."

"Heavens, don't worry about it. I think under the circumstances Manchester can afford a package of croissants." She gave instructions to the waiter, who nodded and went back to the kitchen. Then she pushed away her plate and rested her arms on the table as she leaned toward Krysta. "Your new book is wonderful."

Krysta didn't think she could be happier if she'd written the outline for *Primary Needs* herself. She beamed at Stephanie. "I hoped you'd like it."

"I love it, which I think you'll figure out when you hear the deal I'm going to offer you. Now, you still don't have representation at this point, right?"

Krysta went on alert. "Should I have?"

"That's entirely up to you, of course. With most authors I'd say yes, but you seem to have a real grasp of the contract process. I guess it's because of your work at Rainier Paper. But I can recommend a few people if you want to consider getting an agent."

"Not at the moment, but maybe eventually." Krysta realized that when Jack revealed himself as Candy Valentine sometime in the future, he might want to hire an agent to negotiate for him. He was far too subjective to do it for himself.

"In that case—" Stephanie paused as the waiter arrived with the wrapped package of croissants and more coffee. She waited for him to leave and Krysta to tuck the package into her tote bag.

In the process Krysta rearranged the tape recorder to make sure it would get all of this very important conversation.

"Here's what Manchester is prepared to offer for *Primary Needs*," Stephanie said. She named a price that was higher than the amount paid for *Uptown Girl*, but not twice the amount, which was the figure Krysta had in mind.

Krysta picked up her coffee cup and took a slow sip. "This book has the potential to outsell *Uptown Girl*," she said.

"Once again, we're speculating. But I think so, too, which is why I went up on the advance."

"Up a little," Krysta added. "But not a lot."

"I think that's safer. For you and for us."

Krysta set her cup down with great care. "I'll take that into consideration. But if I agree to that amount, I want a raise in the royalty percentage."

Stephanie blinked. Then she leaned back and grinned at Krysta. "Maybe you *should* get an agent. I think I'd come out ahead."

Krysta smiled back. "And I also want a guaranteed advertising budget equal to the advance."

"You do realize that with this first book we're exceeding that."

"Yes, but that doesn't address what you'll do with the second book, does it?"

"Okay." Stephanie leaned forward. "One percentage point higher on the royalty rates, the advance I stated, and an advertising budget of at least that amount, although I suspect it will be higher. We'll want to ride this Valentine's Day promotion for at least another year. Do we have a deal?"

Krysta had her mouth open to agree to the terms when she remembered that hadn't been the plan. "It sounds very good," she said. "But if you don't mind, I'd like a few hours alone in my suite to think it over."

Stephanie looked surprised, but she quickly composed her features. "Of course. We can have dinner tonight and finalize everything then."

"That would be perfect."

"There is another matter I wanted to ask you about, but it can wait until tonight, if you'd like to get back to your hotel."

Krysta wanted to take as much information to Jack as possible. "Now is fine. What is it?"

"Did you pick out your favorite photos for the dust jacket?"

"Uh—" The last thing Krysta remembered about the stack of proofs was that Jack had taken them away from her, dropped them to the floor and pushed her back onto the mattress so that he could... She tried to wipe the vivid image from her mind. "No, not yet," she said hastily, and hoped the strained quality of her voice wasn't obvious to Stephanie.

Stephanie grinned. "Forgot about them while you were watching those movies, didn't you?"

"Yes. I'm sorry. I'll be sure to—"

"Doesn't matter." Stephanie waved a hand in dismissal. "Tonight's fine, since nothing would happen with them until Monday, anyway. But marketing got a set of those proofs, too. That, combined with meeting you, has convinced them we need to put you on tour for *Uptown Girl.*"

As Jack drank coffee and munched on chocolate chip cookies from the honor bar, he wished he could figure out the next step with Krysta. These few days in New York had thrown them together in a crucible of fiery emotions, but it was something like a shipboard romance, minus the ship. Forty-five stories above Times Square in a suite neither of them could afford on their own was far removed from life in Evergreen, Washington. Krysta didn't give him credit for practicality, but he could be far more practical than she guessed.

Dressed only in his jeans, he paced the area in front of the windows and studied the traffic below every few minutes to watch for limos. It was a stupid exercise because limos were everywhere on the streets of New York. Seeing one near the hotel meant nothing, but watching for them gave him something to do.

He'd love to tell Krysta exactly how he felt and ask her to marry him, but that would be pretty selfish at this point. If Hamilton never suspected she'd found somebody else, she might be able to let him down gradually and still get that promotion she needed to finance her dad's care. But Hamilton might become vindictive if he discovered she'd turned right around and chosen a guy from shipping over him. He might even arrange to get her fired.

That wouldn't matter if Jack could be assured he was about to earn a ton of money. Yet no matter what grandiose predictions Manchester made, nobody knew how the book would sell until it hit the stores next year. He'd read enough industry magazines to get that message loud and clear. Candy Valentine was still a huge gamble and would be for many months to come.

He wandered into the bedroom yet again to check the time on Krysta's travel alarm. She'd been gone a very long two hours and he was going crazy waiting for her. Of course he was eager to hear about Manchester's reaction to his new book, but he'd been thinking about making love to Krysta far more than he'd been thinking about another book deal. He'd even put a condom in his jeans pocket so he didn't have to waste time looking for one. And still he had no answers about their future.

Finally he heard her card key in the lock. Heart pounding in anticipation, he set his coffee cup on the banquet table and walked over to meet her. Soul-searching would just have to wait.

She came in the door, a glorious smile on her face. "Jack, I have some wonderful—"

"Everything about you is wonderful." He captured her with one arm around her waist, took the tote bag with his other hand and kicked the door shut with his foot. "And I need all of it right this minute." He dropped the tote bag to the floor.

"Wait. I—"

"Can't." His hungry mouth came down on hers as he maneuvered her out of her green jacket and toward the middle of the room. She tasted better than any woman he'd ever kissed. He could live off of her kisses.

When the jacket was free he tossed it over his shoulder and started on the buttons of her blouse.

She framed his face in both hands and pushed his mouth slightly away from hers. "Jack, I think you'll want to hear—"

"I want to hear you whimper," he said, pulling the blouse from the waistband of her slacks. "And then I want to hear you cry out when I come inside you." He unfastened the catch on her bra and filled his hands with her breasts.

She moaned and closed her eyes. "Don't say I didn't try to tell you."

"I won't. Unsnap my jeans, Krysta. I need your hands on me."

She hadn't pulled his jeans all the way off by the time he'd slid her slacks and panties to the floor, but she'd accomplished enough to make everything possible. He guided her down to the carpet. Kneeling between her thighs he feasted on the silky warmth of her breasts. Sure enough, there was the whimper he'd been waiting all morning to hear. Rocking back on his heels he gazed at her as he retrieved the condom and put it on.

Lying there, pink and panting and disheveled, she was everything he'd ever dreamed of in a woman, in a lover, in a lifelong mate. Bracing his hands on either side of her, he lowered his hips and plunged deep, rejoicing that she was as hot and wet as if he'd spent hours touching her. With only a few swift strokes he was ready to explode. He gauged the level of passion in her green eyes and decided to go for it. One more thrust and she arched beneath him with the cry of completion he'd longed to hear. He emptied himself inside her with a groan wrenched from the depths of his soul.

Some time later, as sanity slowly returned, they abandoned their place on the carpet, gathered up their clothes and settled themselves in the king-size bed.

He stretched out beside her feeling sated, although he assumed the feeling wouldn't last long. He sighed. "That's better."

She smiled. "Better than what?"

"Anything. Making love to you is better than anything in the world."

"You may not think so when you hear my news."

"I'll still think so. But you might as well tell me this all-fired important info that you thought was more critical than a rendezvous on the rug. I don't want it to interrupt the proceedings again."

She lifted her eyebrows. "There will be more proceedings?"

"I believe there will be. So tell me. What did Stephanie have to say?"

"She loved the new book."

"That's great." Funny how anticlimactic it was after what he'd just shared with Krysta.

"You don't seem very excited, Jack." There was censure in her tone.

He positioned himself so he could nibble at her lower lip. "My priorities have changed."

"She offered more money, but not as much as I thought you deserved."

Jack leaned his forehead against hers and sighed. "Here we go."

"But I think we should take it, because I negotiated a one percent raise in royalty rates and a guaranteed advertising budget in the amount of the advance."

He wondered if she realized how she'd phrased that. *I think we should take it.* Part of him was overjoyed at the sense of commitment that implied, but the other part was terrified she was expecting too much from this fledgling career of his. It wasn't strong enough to keep them both afloat. Not yet, in any case.

"You're not saying anything, Jack. I think it's a good deal."

He raised his head and looked into her eyes. "It's a very good deal. Thank you. Getting a higher royalty percentage is a real coup. You do know your contracts, lady."

"There is one other thing. It has to do with *Uptown Girl.*"

"I'll bet she asked you about that dust jacket picture. I remembered we hadn't picked one out while I was mucking out the bedroom and found the proofs on the floor."

"Stephanie did mention that, but I can tell her what pictures we've chosen when she and I have dinner tonight."

He frowned. "Do you really have to go to dinner with her? I was hoping—"

"I have to give her an answer about the contract, don't forget."

He'd thought they might take a walk through Manhattan tonight. It would be their last chance to do anything like that considering that the plane left first thing in the morning. Maybe by then he'd have worked out a strategy for them to spend time together during the next year without getting either of them fired. "Phone her."

She shook her head. "No, Jack. Now is not the time to appear unfriendly."

He approached her delicious mouth again. "I can testify that you're definitely not unfriendly."

"She wants Candy to go on tour for *Uptown Girl* next February."

He paused a fraction away from her delectable lips. "I hope you told her it was impossible."

"Actually, I told her I probably would."

His head came up again. "You did what?"

"I'm sure there's a way we can manage it. And I think without the tour the whole deal might go sour. I—"

"No." Dammit. Dammit to hell. He'd hoped to avoid a moment like this for a long time. If nothing else was required of her he could have somehow tried to keep the connection between them for the next year until he could be more certain of his publishing career. But this proposal of Stephanie's changed everything. He couldn't ask Krysta to jeopardize her career by making a commitment to go traipsing over the country masquerading as him. The outcome was too uncertain.

"What do you mean, *no?*"

"I mean you're not touring for me."

"Why not?"

"Because I won't ask it of you, and that's that."

12

KRYSTA WAS STUNNED at Jack's reaction. "Of course you can ask it of me! I would be happy to do that for you. Or have I embarrassed you so much during this trip that you can't trust me to represent you on tour?"

Pain flashed in his blue eyes as he reached for her. "No, no. Never that."

"Because I realize I haven't been perfect at this Candy Valentine business." She stumbled over the words, her heart aching because he wouldn't accept her help. "Just this morning Stephanie caught me smuggling croissants, which probably didn't improve Candy's image, and I know you think I'm too tough with the negotiations, but I'm only trying to protect your—"

He pulled her close and gazed earnestly into her eyes. "Krysta, you've been wonderful. We haven't discussed it, but I know you've put your job at risk by coming here. If Hamilton finds out you lied about the spa trip to spend the weekend with me, he might figure out a way to fire you. I'm sure he could dig up some ancient company policy about sexual relations among employees, even if he'd planned to violate the rule himself."

"He's not going to find out."

"I don't plan that he will, either. I'm prepared to go to great lengths to prevent his finding out. But if you went on tour, I'd have to go with you, and that will be nearly impossible to keep secret."

That was the part she'd looked forward to with the most relish. In fact, floating through the hours in a haze of love, she'd even dreamed that they might be married by then. It could all work out so perfectly that way. She'd keep her job at Rainier as insurance for a while, but she didn't expect to need it very long after Jack's first royalty check arrived.

Then gradually Manchester could discover that Candy had a writing assistant named Jack Killigan, and eventually they could learn the true author of the books so Jack could get his rightful measure of praise. Money wouldn't be a problem, because she was a good negotiator, a function she'd continue to fulfill, and Jack was a tremendous writer. They'd be a great team, and knowing Jack's generous nature, she knew her father would be provided for, as well.

"Maybe we wouldn't have to keep the trip secret," she ventured. "I could pretend I'd written the books for as long as you wanted to keep up the pretense, and then we could announce the truth when you were ready."

"And commit career suicide yourself? How long do you think Hamilton or his buddies would want to keep you on if they believed your heart belonged to the publishing world? He'd still be smarting from your rejection, and he'd just love to be able to question your dedication to the company in light of your new interest in becoming a bestselling author. He'd start documenting every slip you made."

She moved away from him. "You're letting that famous imagination of yours run away with you. You don't know that anything of the kind would happen."

"Don't I?"

Privately she had to admit he'd made some valid points. What hurt the most was his apparent refusal to consider the obvious—getting married and sharing in the success of Candy Valentine. But in order to propose marriage to someone you needed to love them, and he'd never spoken those words to her. Words were his strength, his magic wand, his sorcerer's power. He'd used words to tempt her into loving him, but he'd withheld the words she most wanted to hear.

Apparently she was only the means to fulfilling a fantasy for Jack. Once he'd discovered what was under the daisy-patterned nightie, he was compelled to move on to more imaginative conquests. She'd never known much about artistic personalities, but she seemed to be learning in the school of hard knocks this weekend.

She turned onto her back and closed her eyes to stem the flow of tears. She would not give him the satisfaction of seeing her cry. She didn't want this scene to end up in a Candy Valentine novel. She swallowed. "What—what would you suggest I say to Stephanie about the tour?"

He put a hand on her bare shoulder. "Krysta."

She opened her eyes and stared at the ceiling. "Everything you said is absolutely on target, Jack. I don't know what I was thinking of. I guess I got carried away with pretending to be you. I wanted it to go on...forever. But of course that's—"

"I wish it could, too."

For the first time since she'd known Jack, she didn't believe him. She figured he was jollying her along, getting her used to the notion that the party was over. Well, she was a grown up and she didn't need that sort of coddling. She, of all people, understood how the world worked. Jack was about to become famous, and he was hesitant about making commitments at a time like this. One never knew where the road to fame would lead. One needed to keep one's options open.

But she had to convince Stephanie to abandon the idea of a book tour for Candy's first novel. She had no clue how to do that. She took a deep breath. "I just need some ideas, Jack. Some reasons why a book tour would be a bad idea."

"All right," he said quietly. "Remind Stephanie that some very successful authors don't tour, like Danielle Steel, for example. Tell her that you think an air of mystery would be as beneficial as having you out there. And if none of that works, tell her you have motion sickness and nothing cures it. Tell her you barfed all the way to New York and you'll probably barf all the way home."

She just might, at that, Krysta thought. She continued to gaze up at the ceiling. "I'll try those things. I can't guarantee that it won't affect the deal, though. She seemed really keen on this idea of a book tour. But I'll do the best I can."

"With you, that's a given." He shifted his weight and moved the upper part of his body over hers, bracing his hand beside her head so that she was forced to look at him. "I want you to know something. I wish circumstances could be different. But you need to hang on to your job at Rainier if you hope to be able to help your father. My future is very...uncertain. I can't have you hitching your wagon to a star that might very quickly fall to earth."

"You won't fall to earth, Jack."

He smiled. "And you're prejudiced."

"Maybe, but I've been hearing what Stephanie says, and you're..." She blinked. The tears were very persistent. "You're really going to make it," she finished, and turned her face toward the pillow.

"Hey," he murmured, touching her cheek. "Please don't—my God, you're crying."

"No, I'm not!"

"Krysta—" He turned her face back toward him. "Krysta, don't." His lips covered hers.

A woman with a stitch of pride would push him away, she thought. So what if his kiss moved like velvet over her bruised lips? So what if he knew just how to comb his fingers through her hair so that she felt treasured for all time? He didn't mean a bit of it. He was a fantasy lover, just like the heroes in his books. He'd needed her to play a part for him, just like he needed the heroines of his novels to play a part each time he started a new book. And now the role was complete. But he wasn't a mean-spirited person, so he didn't want her to feel sad about it. She just wished she could stop crying.

"Hush, Krysta," he crooned, taking her more fully into his arms. "It's been a rough few days. Everything will be okay. I've expected too much. I'm sorry. There, now. I'm right here."

Which only made her cry harder. Of course he was right here. But after tomorrow, when the plane took them back to Washington, where would he be? Oh, she might see him in the company cafeteria now and then, but soon he'd leave Rainier to write full time and become a bestselling author. And she would be a memory. A sweet memory, perhaps, but part of his past, part of his beginnings, before he became rich and famous.

"Krysta," he murmured, kissing her damp cheeks. "Please, sweetheart. Please don't cry."

She could only think of one way to make herself stop. Taking his head in both hands, she brought his mouth down on hers. She might not have Jack Killigan for long, but she had him now.

He needed very little urging to make love to her again. At least she still had the power to ignite his lust, she thought with some gratitude. Maybe there was even a little bit of love mixed in there, too. She imagined there was as she gazed into his blue, blue eyes while he moved gently within her. Funny how she'd once thought Jack was beneath her notice. Now he seemed beyond her reach.

JACK FELT LIKE a first-class heel. Damn Stephanie Briggs for making it seem as if Candy Valentine was only a step away from the *New York Times* bestseller list. Damn Stephanie for suggesting a book tour for Candy, which forced him to take a protective stance with Krysta, who naively thought he was a shoo-in for fame and fortune. He could try to tell her his future as a novelist was far from secure. But he was quite sure he could tell her until the cows came home, and she'd never believe him after the way she'd been dazzled by Manchester. She thought he was putting her off, delaying a commitment, because he didn't care enough. The truth was he cared too much.

So because he didn't feel free to say it all—that he loved her and wanted to spend the rest of his life with her—he said nothing. Instead, he spent the rest of that day giving her pleasure and praying that she'd absorb the depth of his caring through his touch. His heart wrenched with the knowledge that she loved him, but felt she couldn't say the words any more than he could. Each of them existed in a self-imposed prison, and the only communication they allowed themselves was a physical expression of desire.

When at last Krysta left for her dinner with Stephanie, Jack had never felt so sexually satisfied in his life. Or so unbearably heartsick.

KRYSTA SAT ACROSS the table from Stephanie within the jeweled interior of Tavern on the Green in the midst of Central Park. From the kaleidoscope of multicolored crystal and stained glass inside to the fairy lights and Chinese lanterns outside, the restaurant sparkled with an intensity befitting Stephanie's vision of Candy Valentine's future.

"Believe me, you're going to be big. Very big," Stephanie said as dessert was served. "But the tour is all part of the plan. We're not just selling the book, we're selling you, and the idea of an author as delicious as a box of chocolates. You're perfect to promote that image. I can't believe you're turning your back on it."

Krysta had tried all of Jack's arguments and none of them had worked with Stephanie. She'd dismissed the Danielle Steel comment as irrelevant in today's market. Steel already had her audience, she'd said. Candy Valentine had to build one, and not by appearing mysterious, but by appearing accessible. When Krysta had finally played her last card, Stephanie had promised to find her a specialist on motion sickness who would certainly cure her of nausea.

Krysta was out of ideas and out of energy. Abandoning the argument for the time being, she pulled the photo proofs from her tote bag and she and Stephanie spent the rest of the time in the restaurant deciding which one to use. They ended up with the shot of Krysta in the full-length coat.

Finally the meal was over and Krysta hoped to be allowed to go back to the hotel with the matter of the tour on hold, at the very least.

"I think I'll just share a taxi with you as far as the Marriott," Stephanie said.

Krysta groaned inwardly, knowing the campaign would continue in the cab. Sure enough, it did.

When the cab driver opened Krysta's door at the hotel entrance, Stephanie got out and paid the fare.

Krysta glanced at her uneasily. "Aren't you taking this cab home?"

"I just had a better idea. How about a nightcap?"

Under the bright lights of the Marriott's portico, Krysta felt as if she were standing on stage and she didn't know any of her lines. "I'm a little tired, Stephanie. Sorry."

"Just one. A brandy would go perfectly right now, don't you think? A farewell toast, so to speak."

No, Krysta didn't think so at all. But Jack's career depended on the goodwill of this woman. She wouldn't get Candy to go on tour, so Krysta decided maybe a farewell toast was required. "Why not?" she said.

"Excellent." Stephanie smiled and took her arm as they walked into the hotel and headed for the elevator.

As they waited for an elevator to be free Krysta turned toward Stephanie. "Would you rather go to the lobby bar or the revolving one on top of the hotel?"

"I think it would be much cozier if we just went up to your suite and ordered room service. I'm interested in what sort of room Manchester reserved for you."

Krysta felt as if Stephanie had just doused her with ice water. "Oh, let's not," she said quickly. "The place is a mess. Truly. I'd hate for you to see what a slob I am."

Stephanie laughed. "What nonsense. I'm not going to be the least bothered with a few articles of clothing lying around."

You might if they belonged to Jack, Krysta thought. She mustn't panic. There was a way out of this. "I haven't been to the rooftop bar yet," she said. "I'd really like to see it."

"Next trip." The elevator arrived and Stephanie walked inside. "Coming?"

Krysta hurried into the elevator after her. "Look, Stephanie, this is a very bad idea. I don't feel well. I think I'm coming down with something. Something contagious."

"I know what your problem is. You're afraid I'll convince you to go on that tour. That I'll wear you down. What floor?"

Krysta panicked. "Stephanie, please—"

Stephanie stood with her hand on the Door Open button, which held the elevator in place. *"What floor, Candy?"*

Krysta hadn't seen this side of Stephanie, the side that wouldn't take no for an answer, but it explained her attaining such a position of power with Manchester

Publishing at a relatively young age. Krysta had the feeling that if she didn't go along with Stephanie and take her up to the room, she might cancel Jack's contract, unreasonable though that might be. "Forty-fifth," she said. "But I insist you give me thirty seconds to pick up the place before I invite you in."

Stephanie punched the button and the glass elevator started up the terraced atrium of the hotel. "Goodness, anyone would think you had a man hiding in your room."

Krysta tried to laugh and started to choke.

Stephanie pounded her on the back. "You *are* a bundle of nerves. A shot of brandy is exactly what you need. I'm glad I thought of it. I know it can be disconcerting, attaining this level of success after years of struggling in obscurity, but I'm going to get you past this paranoia, Candy. I've been dealing with authors for years. You're not the first one to run screaming from the thought of doing a little publicity."

Krysta sank against the elevator wall and tried to imagine how she'd get out of this mess.

Stephanie crossed her arms and gazed at her. "I used to be just like you, afraid of success, but I conquered that fear and I've never looked back. You're going to thank me someday for giving you a little push, Ms. Candy Valentine."

Krysta resisted the urge to laugh, afraid that she'd lose control and lapse into hysteria. For the first time she understood how Jack must have felt during all those lectures she'd given him in the Rainier cafeteria, and how she must have sounded to her brothers over the years she'd helped raise them. Stephanie was using exactly the same tone, and it made Krysta feel like a wayward child. She didn't much like the experience.

The elevator doors slid open at the forty-fifth floor and Krysta hurried out. "Don't forget. I get thirty seconds to tidy the place up."

"To tell the truth, I'm not surprised you're worried about that. You have definite perfectionistic tendencies. I can see it in your work."

"You can?" Now that was something to think about. Surely Jack didn't have perfectionistic tendencies. Or did he? Perhaps she'd been too blinded by her own assessment of him to notice.

She dug in her tote bag for the key as she tried to outdistance Stephanie. It didn't work. Stephanie's long stride kept right up with her even though she was practically running down the corridor. She pushed the card key into the slot and prayed that Jack wouldn't meet her at the door.

"Be right with you, Stephanie," she said, a little louder than necessary as she opened the door about a foot. She slipped through and slammed the door in the editor's face.

Jack leaped up from the couch and threw down the book he'd been reading. "Who?"

She rushed over to him. "Keep your voice down," she muttered. "She insisted on coming up to the room for a nightcap."

He stared at her.

"I tried to avoid it, Jack, believe me. Finally, I was afraid she'd cancel the whole deal if I didn't let her come up here. And I've used all your arguments against the tour. She's not buying a single one of them."

"Do you think she's on to us?" he murmured.

"I don't think so. I hope not. Just take your book and go hide in the bedroom. I'll get rid of her as soon as I can."

"Right. And don't agree to that damn tour, no matter how many nightcaps you have."

She put her hands on her hips. "I am not in the habit of getting drunk and giving in."

"Yeah, I know. I tried that." With one last glance, he went into the bedroom and closed the door.

Krysta took a quick inventory of the suite and was about to let Stephanie in when she saw Jack's running shoes lying beside a chair. No way could she explain size twelve Reeboks. She grabbed them and ran to the bedroom door. She flung it open and heaved them in the general direction of the bed where Jack lay reading. As she closed the door she realized that Jack had been forced to duck. And maybe she'd meant for him to.

Taking a deep breath, she walked to the hall door and opened it.

ONCE HE HEARD VOICES out in the living room, Jack left the bed and went over to sit on the floor beside the door and listen as best he could to the conversation. Krysta was ticked. She'd heaved those shoes right at him, and he didn't think it was an accident.

Hell, he didn't blame her for being furious. He'd started something he wasn't in a position to finish. Yet during the evening as he'd waited for her to come back, he'd been unable to dredge up any regret for what had happened in the past three days. All his fantasies about Krysta had come true except the part about living happily ever after, and he wasn't giving up on that one yet, although he couldn't tell her.

As for Krysta, he didn't think she'd settle for somebody like Derek Hamilton after this weekend, and that was a plus. Jack might still lose her to somebody with a better portfolio, because she had to consider her responsibilities to her father. But at least now she'd demand a guy who knew something about how to treat a woman. He hadn't allowed himself to contemplate the idea of her with someone else, though, which had served the useful purpose of keeping him from punching holes in the hotel walls.

He leaned against the door and heard Krysta order a bottle of very good brandy from room service. He shouldn't have made that crack about having too many nightcaps and agreeing to the book tour. She would never allow herself to get tipsy under these circumstances and he knew it.

The stupid remark indicated how frustrated he was becoming with the whole situation, but that didn't excuse it. He'd apologize after Stephanie left. Then maybe he'd ask if he could keep seeing Krysta once they returned to Evergreen, although they'd have to be careful not to run afoul of Hamilton for a while. Maybe if Jack kept coming around, she'd begin to understand that he wasn't avoiding a commitment, just postponing it until the right time.

He concentrated on the conversation between Stephanie and Krysta, and from what he could tell it centered around an illuminated billboard visible from the hotel window. He vaguely remembered the billboard, a shirtless guy who was modeling designer jeans.

"Looks like a candidate for a Candy Valentine hero to me," Stephanie said clearly.

"He is pretty cute, at that," Krysta said, almost as if she'd raised her voice for his benefit. "Nice pecs."

Jack gritted his teeth. She sure knew how to get under his skin.

"You should see some of the cover models," Stephanie said. "Really yummy. I already have somebody in mind for Jake in *Uptown Girl*. I think we'll show him shirtless, like that guy on the billboard."

"I can see that for the cover," Krysta said.

"You know, it would be fun if you could be around for the cover shoot. Hey, maybe you'd like to meet the model I have in mind. You two would probably hit it off great."

"Sounds nice, but we'll have to see," Krysta said.

Jack's breath hissed out through his teeth. He could have done without the sounds *nice* part.

"Do you have a guy waiting for you back home, Candy?"

Jack tensed.

"No, nobody," Krysta said.

Jack leaned his head back and closed his eyes. *Nobody*. But there was, dammit. She just didn't understand.

The brandy arrived, and there was some clinking of glasses and laughter as they apparently got comfortable with their nightcaps.

"I'm just not going to take no for an answer on that book tour," Stephanie said. "You're doing it, and that's that."

"I really can't," Krysta replied.

"All right. I didn't want to play hardball, but you're

forcing me to. Unless you agree to the book tour, we'll have to reconsider our publishing program for you. We need that tour to help assure Candy Valentine's success. You scratch our back, we'll scratch yours. That's the way it has to be."

Jack surged to his feet, ready to go out and tell Stephanie what she could do with her program. His hand was on the knob as Krysta gave her answer.

"Then, of course I'll do the tour."

13

JACK FROZE IN PLACE. She was willing to make that kind of sacrifice for him, even if she thought he didn't care enough to offer her a wedding ring? He'd get her out of the tour somehow, of course, but if he stormed out there now he'd diminish the value of her gesture and make her look like a fool in front of Stephanie.

"I'm glad you came to your senses," Stephanie said. "Now, before I leave, I'd like to use your bathroom, if I may."

Grabbing his shoes, Jack headed for the closet with no time to scan the place for any other signs of his presence, but he had a bad feeling that a pair of Jockey shorts were lying somewhere on the floor. He had to crouch down to fit under the top shelf, but he managed to close the closet door after him before Stephanie walked into the bedroom. From what he could tell, Krysta was right on her heels.

"Now you'll really embarrass me," Krysta said. "I'm sure the bathroom is a disaster."

Jack could picture Krysta, her heart pounding as she visually swept the area.

"I'm not on an inspection tour," Stephanie said. Then the bathroom door closed.

Jack stood with Krysta's white silk blouse caressing his cheek on one side and the powder-blue suit she'd worn on the plane rubbing his shoulder on the other side. The whole closet was filled with her fragrance, and he wanted to hold her so much his arms ached.

"Jack," Krysta whispered from just outside the closet. "You in there?"

"Yeah," he whispered back. "Did you find anything of mine on the floor?"

"I kicked your Jockey shorts under the bed. Jack, I had to agree to the tour."

"I know."

There was the sound of the bathroom door opening again. "Krysta?" Stephanie said. "Are you okay?"

Krysta's footsteps headed away from him. "I'm fine," she said. "Why?"

"When I came out, I could have sworn you were talking to the closet."

"Just verbally going over my wardrobe," Krysta said. "Making sure I had something to wear back on the plane."

"With the closet door closed?"

"That's right. You caught me standing there muttering to myself. Authors are strange ducks, as I'm sure you've discovered over the years."

"You're right, I have. By the way, I noticed you use a man's razor and shaving cream on your legs. I've found that works better, too."

"Yes, it certainly does." Krysta closed the bedroom door after them.

Still holding his shoes, Jack emerged cautiously from the closet and crept over to listen at the door again. Stephanie seemed to be in the process of taking her leave, thank God.

"It's been a fascinating few days," Stephanie said. "I feel as if we're very much alike, you and I."

"I think so, too," Krysta agreed.

There was a pause. "You're sure you don't have a special someone back in Evergreen?"

"Yes, I'm very sure."

"Then maybe that special someone is right here in New York with you?"

"I—I don't know what you mean," Krysta stammered.

Jack held his breath.

"Don't be embarrassed about it," Stephanie said. "I probably would have brought my boyfriend along for support on my first trip to New York. But next time, come alone. You're a big girl now, and you can make your own business decisions."

"Stephanie, I—"

"With the kind of drive you've shown thus far, it didn't make sense to me that you'd fight the idea of a tour so vigorously, especially after you indicated originally that you'd do it. Besides that, the arguments you came up with sounded a little rehearsed. Finally, I put all the evidence together and came up with the answer. I've edited a fair amount of mysteries in my day, too."

Her comment was met with dead silence. Jack could imagine Krysta standing there completely dumbstruck.

"Some men can't handle it when their women threaten to become independent and successful," Stephanie continued. "If this guy of yours is telling you it's okay to make a lot of money, but not okay to get out there and promote your book, please don't listen to him. Soon you'll have your pick of gorgeous men. You don't have to settle for a chauvinist."

"I—I'll keep that in mind."

"And I'll be in touch. It's been a pleasure, Candy. Good night, now."

Jack slumped against the doorjamb and waited until Krysta came and opened the bedroom door.

She stood there, looking exhausted. "Did you hear her? She thinks Candy Valentine was bush-league enough to drag her hometown sweetheart to New York with her. And that he's the reason she won't go on tour."

"He is."

Tired though she obviously was, Krysta lifted her chin in defiance. "Well, too bad. I'm going on that tour. This whole house of cards will collapse if I don't. Furthermore, I see no reason why you have to come along. I've got the routine down well enough. It's not as if I have to speak in literary phrases or anything. Maybe I'll even take a community college course in literature, just to beef up my conversation on the subject of writing and writers."

He rolled his eyes. "You're crazy. You don't have the time to—"

"I believe in finishing what I start, as I've said to you before. When the tour is over and your first book is a success, you can decide what to do about the entire charade. But if I don't do this for *Uptown Girl* next February, your career won't be launched."

"Sure it will. Maybe not with as much fanfare, but the book will still be published. Stephanie won't change her mind about that."

"Maybe not, but she'll think Candy is a wimp who listens to her boyfriend instead of standing on her own two feet."

"Who cares what Stephanie thinks?"

"Well, you should, but that's only part of the problem with not doing the tour. I realize after this very informative weekend that it takes more than a good book to make somebody a bestseller. You may never have such a golden opportunity to get your work in front of an audience as you do right now. I don't want your failure as a writer on my conscience."

Her tone was reminiscent of the lectures she used to give him in the Rainier cafeteria, but tonight he wasn't amused. He was frustrated as hell at her bullheadedness. "Krysta, think of the consequences to you. You'll have to lie to Hamilton again, and this time it will be an even bigger lie. You'll have to pretend you're going on a book tour for your first book, because the word might easily get back to him if you're going to be that visible. And you'll have to tell the same lie to your friends and your family. Everybody you know will be led to believe that you're Candy Valentine. That's nuts."

"In your view. Not in mine. Now, if you'll excuse me, I'd like to go to bed. We have a plane to catch in the morning."

The ice dripping from her every syllable told him that she intended to go to bed alone.

He lost control. "You're being a damned martyr, Krysta! Hamilton will crucify you and you'll be left with nothing! What about your career? What about your father?"

A dangerous-looking light came into her green eyes. "I can handle Derek, Jack."

His blood ran cold. There was only one way he could imagine her handling Derek Hamilton. He'd been so sure she wouldn't settle for a guy like that, but maybe he'd been wrong. "Don't do it, Krysta."

The crack of her hand against his cheek resounded in the stillness that followed. "How dare you?" she whispered at last, her whole body trembling.

As he stared into the fury and hurt of her gaze, he had no answer. And where Krysta was concerned, he had no rights, either, considering he wasn't ready to step forward to claim her himself. "Okay, maybe that was out of line."

"*Maybe?*" She stormed past him into the bedroom.

"Okay, it was definitely out of line." He couldn't demand that she not go back to Hamilton. He could only hope she wouldn't.

She paused by the bedside table with her back to him. When she turned around she had something in her hand, and tears were streaming down her cheeks. "Here, Jack. Catch!" She hurled the plastic heart across the room.

He caught it with one hand and the plastic arrow shaft bit into his palm.

"Now get out of my sight."

He left the room, and walked out of the suite. Outside in the hall he paused to put on his shoes. His jacket was still inside, but he didn't care. He trotted toward the emergency exit door and pounded down the stairs, the downward spiral perfectly matching his mood. Once outside he hit the pavement running, welcoming the cold. As he ran he tried to crush the fear that he'd just hurled Krysta right back into Derek Hamilton's arms.

BY THE TIME KRYSTA opened her bedroom door the next morning, Jack was already packed and gone. Somehow he also avoided her in the airline terminal. Although the flight home was a blur of pain as she worked to blot out thoughts of the man sitting back in the coach section, she forced herself to think through her options.

If she planned very carefully, she would get her promotion, provide for her father's care and do Jack's book tour. It was a lot to handle, but if she'd learned one thing in life, it was how to shoulder responsibility. Because she had no intention of becoming a martyr or Derek's mistress, she had to find a way to make herself more valuable to Rainier Paper.

Her first move after returning to work on Monday morning was to pay a visit to marketing department head Denise Terkel to present some of the ideas she'd picked up while schmoozing with the marketing department at Manchester. Advertising was advertising, in her opinion, and it was time she concentrated on a transfer to a department where promotion was more likely.

"EXCELLENT IDEAS, KRYSTA." Denise, a redheaded dynamo who stood barely five feet tall, smiled at Krysta across the cluttered expanse of her desk. "Did you dream those up while you were soaking in a mud bath at that spa you went to?"

"You might say that."

"I didn't realize we had such a creative mind sitting down in the contracts department."

Krysta absorbed that statement and its possible implications. "I guess you've forgotten I was the one who suggested doing infomercials promoting Rainier's research into alternative sources of paper material," she said carefully.

Denise frowned. "I thought that was Derek Hamilton's idea."

So Derek hadn't given her credit. No wonder there had been no action on her request for a transfer to advertising. "Well, we sort of brainstormed it together," she said. "He must have forgotten to mention that."

Denise steepled her fingers and gazed at Krysta over the tips of her manicured nails. "I guess he must have."

"I'd really love to work in this department, Denise."

"Considering that you're a bundle of innovation, I don't see why that can't be arranged. Juliet won't be happy to lose you in contracts, but Rainier likes to make the most of an employee's potential."

"That's good news. Now I'd better get back to my post." With a firm handshake, she left Denise's office and went straight to Derek's. He was in a meeting, so she left word for him to call her.

By lunchtime she still hadn't heard from Derek. She went out to a small café with Rosie rather than chance going down to the cafeteria and running into Jack. He had transformed her entire view of the world, but the less she saw of him now, the better. Her wounds were still too fresh.

When she and Rosie returned there was a message on her desk from Derek, who said he'd pick her up at six for dinner. She tried to reach him for the rest of the afternoon to beg off, but he was never available. Finally, she decided to have dinner with him, after all. At least she'd be able to confront him about taking credit for her idea. She'd handle it diplomatically, of course, but she couldn't just let it go.

At her apartment after work she dressed carefully in a modest black knit and pearls. She'd told Jack she would handle Derek, and Derek himself had given her the means. He probably never imagined she would talk to Denise about the infomercial. Assuming he'd taken credit for her idea, which Krysta was pretty sure he had, she could express disappointment but let him know she hadn't spilled the beans to Denise. But she'd use his behavior to put him on the defensive so he couldn't object when she ended their relationship.

Derek arrived promptly at six, every hair in place, his topcoat over his arm and his navy blazer free of even the slightest speck of lint.

Krysta marveled that she'd once found his brand of faultless grooming attractive. She picked up her coat and purse from a hall table near the door. "I'm ready."

"Before we go, I have something to discuss with you." Derek moved past her into her small apartment's tiny living room, which held only two chairs, one lamp and a television set.

"All right." Krysta put down her coat and purse and closed the front door. "I have something to discuss with you, as well." Maybe she wouldn't have to sit through a dinner with him, after all.

He laid his topcoat carefully over the back of a chair. "If you don't mind, I'd like to go first. I did a little checking and discovered you went to New York City this past weekend."

She was instantly on guard. She wasn't sure how he'd found that out, but she'd might as well not deny it. "The spa was outside the city, but I flew in there, yes."

He gazed at her. "Jack Killigan was on that same plane. Did you know that?"

She tried her best to stay calm. "Really? What a co-incidence."

"Don't dig yourself in deeper, Krysta." He approached her slowly, like a cat stalking its prey. "You've had lunch with the guy on a regular basis and you told me he comes from your hometown. I'm not going to buy the story that you didn't know he was on that plane with you. I have only one question. Are you and Killigan having an affair?"

"No." It was the absolute truth.

He stepped closer. "That was uttered with conviction, which gladdens my heart." He put his hands on her shoulders and gazed into her eyes. "What happened? Did you discover a common laborer wasn't the kind of man you wanted in your bed?"

She brushed his hands aside and stepped back. "I demand an apology for that remark, Derek."

He shrugged. "All right. I apologize. But you'll have to forgive me for being upset. For weeks you've been putting me off every time I tried to get close to you, and then I discover you've apparently run away for a weekend rendezvous with one of the dock workers. So if you're not having an affair with him, what's the story? How did you two end up on the same plane?"

Fear for Jack roiled in her stomach. Derek wouldn't hesitate to fire Jack, who could be replaced easily. He might not be so quick to get rid of her, because she was an important part of the daily operation and he knew it. His superiors would demand reasons for her dismissal, but they wouldn't give a second thought about Jack. Her brain felt like a pan of scrambled eggs.

"Jack had no part in it," she said, desperate to come up with a plausible story that would take the pressure off the man she loved. "I found out he was going to New York to see a friend from college, and I booked myself on the same plane." She laughed. "All my life I've gone out with brainy guys like you, Derek. But lots of women, me included, have a fantasy about the brawny type. I thought I might talk Jack into satisfying that fantasy. But he turned me down flat."

Derek came close again and placed his hands at her waist. "You know what? Crazy as that story sounds, I believe you. I've always sensed something wild and rebellious in you trying to get out." His thumbs kneaded her waist.

She tried not to shudder, or worse yet, become sick to her stomach.

"I can satisfy that wildness, Krysta, if you'll only let me."

In your dreams, Charlie. She tried to ease away, but he gripped her harder.

"It's time, Krysta," he murmured, trying to bring her closer. "I can't have you prowling around after dock workers when I can take care of all your needs."

"Let go of me!" Unable to stand his touch another second, she wrenched away.

He started after her. "Now, let's not be shy. We both know what you want."

She clenched her jaw. This wasn't going well. "I'm sorry, Derek. I'm not interested in having a physical relationship with you."

He paused, looking genuinely puzzled. "But I thought we were getting along, you and I."

"We were—are. Were. But not in that respect. I admired you as a colleague but found that romantically we...just didn't click. Then today I discovered that you apparently presented the infomercial idea to marketing as yours alone."

His face turned pink. "So that's it. You're mad at me because of that. Okay, I'll go back and tell them you had some part in it, if that's all you want. Denise called me today and asked me to approve your transfer to marketing. I'll recommend you for it. Happy now?"

She took a deep breath. "Thank you."

He took a step toward her. "You can do a hell of a lot better than a mere thank you, Krysta."

Jack's warning rang in her ears. She hadn't wanted to believe him. "Surely you don't expect that I'll go to bed with you because you're treating me with the consideration every employee deserves?"

"Now, that would be crass of me, wouldn't it?"

Relief swept through her and she smiled. "I knew you wouldn't—"

"I expect you to go to bed with me because we belong together. We're two of a kind, and it's about time you recognized the fact."

"I disagree. We don't belong together. I'm sorry, Derek, but we really don't."

He grabbed her before she realized what he intended to do. Holding her with a strength that surprised her, he shoved his face close to hers. "You stubborn little bitch. You obviously don't know what's good for you, but I'm going to try and teach you the error of your ways. Either we go into that bedroom now, or your story about chasing to New York after Killigan goes in your file, along with every single mistake you make from here on out. You'll be gone in three months."

She curled her hands into fists to keep from scraping

her nails across his face. She'd save that for later if she needed it. "I won't be gone in three months, Derek," she said, her voice quivering.

His expression cleared. "Now you're making sense."

"I'm gone now." She pushed with all her might, and the element of surprise freed her from his grip. "I resign."

He stood and stared at her. "You're crazy."

"You're not the first person to tell me that recently." She felt a wonderful sense of freedom. Later remorse would probably hit full force, but at the moment she felt glorious.

"I know how much you need this job."

"Not that much. Don't let the door hit you on the way out, Derek."

He snatched his topcoat from the chair and stomped past her. "You'll regret this."

"Probably, but right now it feels fabulous."

His response was to slam the door so hard her living room window rattled.

Krysta gazed at the door and wondered why she didn't feel grief-stricken at having just sawed off the limb she was sitting on. Jobs weren't that easy to come by in this neck of the woods. Instead of a bigger paycheck to help pay for her father's care, she had no paycheck.

Yet something deep inside told her she'd done the right thing, both for her and for her family. Self-annihilation didn't set a very good example for her brothers. She'd try to get a job that paid better than the one at Rainier, but if she couldn't, she and her brothers would work things out. Having Stephanie take charge of her life in the same way she'd so often taken charge of her brothers' lives had been an illuminating experience. Perhaps she needed to allow her brothers the freedom to make their own decisions about their education and helping out with their father.

And if she didn't get a job, there was another consideration. She'd have plenty of time to go on tour for Candy Valentine.

14

"I STILL SAY IT'S LAWSUIT time." Rosie stood, feet braced and hands on her hips as she watched Krysta clean out her desk. "In case you haven't noticed, it's not quite so easy for men to get away with sexual harassment in the workplace these days."

"I'll think about it." Krysta put her family beach picture into a cardboard box before glancing up at Rosie. "But it was only one incident, and there were no witnesses, so it could turn into a 'he said, she said' kind of thing. I went out with him for several months, so building a case might be tough."

"I still think you should try. I know it's easy for me to say, but if we don't stop the Derek Hamiltons of the world, who will?"

"You're right. I really will think about it." Krysta regretted telling Rosie that she was quitting because Derek had demanded sexual favors in exchange for a promotion. It was the nearest to the truth she could come with Rosie, who had been a good friend and didn't deserve to be stonewalled. But Krysta hadn't made any reference to Jack. A lawsuit against Derek would undoubtedly result in unmasking Jack as the real Candy Valentine. A court case was out of the question under the circumstances, but she couldn't tell Rosie why.

"I wish Juliet hadn't picked this week to go over to

China and finalize the adoption of her little girl. She'd back you on this, and she's got clout with the rest of the brass."

Krysta interwove the flaps on the box. Then she addressed her friend with great care. "Don't forget that what I told you is confidential. I don't want anyone else to know about Derek's behavior."

"I promised, and I won't break that promise, but the whole thing stinks, if you ask me."

Krysta rolled back her chair and stood. "Try looking at it from a different angle. Maybe, now that I'm free of Rainier, there's a better job waiting for me out there, one with greater chances for—"

"I don't even want to hear it. I believe if some cloud showed up without a silver lining, you'd have it recalled. Don't you ever get mad and just want to punch the hell out of someone?"

Krysta remembered vividly the last time that had happened. She'd hit the man she loved. "That doesn't solve anything, Rosie."

"Maybe not, but it sure can make you feel better."

"Not necessarily." She walked over to the coatrack.

"Then that's where you and I are different, Mother Teresa. Don't forget we're going out tonight for a cholesterol binge. I'll pick you up right after I blow this miserable joint at five."

Krysta walked over and gave Rosie a hug. "Don't let my experience sour you on Rainier. It's a good company, and except for Derek, the management's the best."

Rosie hugged her back. "And we're gonna get that SOB sooner or later."

"Yeah." Krysta decided to leave it at that. "See you

tonight." She was almost out the door with her box when Rosie called after her.

"Are you gonna go say goodbye to Jack Killigan?"

Just the mention of his name almost made her drop the box. She sure hoped Derek hadn't started rumors about her already. "Why?"

Rosie's expression was innocent. "Just wondering. He's a nice guy, and he seems to think a lot of you."

"Then maybe I will stop by the shipping dock before I leave." On the way out to her car in the drizzle of a February afternoon, she contemplated the wisdom of going to see Jack. She didn't intend to tell him she'd quit, just that she'd arranged the time off for his book tour. Because they were avoiding each other these days, he wouldn't discover her absence at Rainier for quite a while.

By the time he did, she'd be set up in a new job, a better job. The last thing in the world she wanted from Jack was pity.

After depositing the box in the passenger seat of her car, she locked the door and trudged back through the rain to the entrance nearest the shipping dock. On her way in she met the foreman, Bud.

"You're here to see Jack, I'll bet," he said.

"That's right."

"I'll get him for you."

Wish you could, Krysta thought wistfully as the foreman walked through the door onto the noisy dock. But Jack Killigan was a shooting star traveling at light speed away from her.

Jack came through the door wearing his blue coveralls and yellow hardhat. Of course, she'd known his hair was short now and his glasses had been replaced with contact lenses, but she still blinked at the transformation it made. Even his movements seemed more purposeful, his gaze more direct. And he was so gorgeous she caught her breath.

He walked toward her. "You've been out in the rain."

All I have to offer is a kiss in the rain. She swallowed the lump in her throat and tried to keep her voice steady. "I had to put some things in my car, and then I decided to stop by and tell you that I'm cleared for the book tour."

"Dammit, Krysta, I didn't want you to—"

"Nobody knows anything about Candy Valentine, Jack. Not yet, at any rate."

His eyes narrowed. "Then how did you get Hamilton to give you that much time off?"

"That's my business."

A muscle worked in his jaw and he swore softly under his breath as he stared up at the ceiling.

She could almost read his mind. He thought she'd slept with Derek to get this favor. But she wouldn't stoop to defending herself against the unspoken accusation.

When his gaze returned to hers, it was bleak. "And now you're all prepared to go on tour for me."

"This is for the best, Jack."

His laugh was bitter. "What a typical rose-colored glasses remark." A pulse throbbed in his temple as he glanced away and his chest heaved. "I had no idea you'd work so fast, but I should have known." He rubbed a hand over his face. "I just wish to hell you'd waited another twenty-four hours. Maybe you can trade that time off for a promotion, or maybe some company stock."

"What are you talking about?"

He glanced back at her. "I called Stephanie Briggs this morning. I tried to get her yesterday, but she wasn't available."

She felt as if she'd just swallowed a large chunk of ice. "Why did you call her?" But she knew. He'd abandoned the charade, abandoned her.

"Turns out it's no big deal, after all, Candy Valentine being a guy," Jack said. "Stephanie and I had a good laugh over it, and everything's cool."

"I see." She'd known her usefulness to him would end someday, but she hadn't expected to be discarded quite so soon. She waited for the heartrending pain to hit, but apparently the news had left her numb. She felt nothing.

"Dammit, Krysta, couldn't you have been a little less efficient?"

At last her anger kicked in. "And couldn't you at least have notified me of your intentions?"

"Couldn't you have notified me of yours?"

Fury bubbled in her veins. "You mean my intentions regarding Derek?"

"Yes." His jaw clenched. "I deserved to know. You can't convince me he blithely gave you three weeks off, months in advance, for no good reason."

"Of course he wouldn't do that." Suddenly she wanted him to believe the worst because it would hurt him, and she wanted him to hurt. "But don't think it was all self-sacrifice on my part. I enjoyed every minute of it."

"Liar! Three days ago we were—"

"I'm not lying." She didn't want to be reminded of what had been happening three days ago. And besides, she was telling Jack the truth. Resigning in the face of Derek's demands had been one of the best experiences of her life. By giving herself more autonomy, she was able to grant more to the members of her family.

Jack looked as if a paper bale had just fallen on him. "I can't believe it," he said tonelessly.

"I'm not one of the heroines of your novels, Jack."

His gaze intensified. "My mistake. Apparently you're not. And it seems that Hamilton is getting exactly what he deserves."

"I think he will. Goodbye, Jack. Best of luck with your writing career." She hurried down the hall and out into the rain.

"DON'T GIVE ME THAT innocent little smile, babe." Jack took a swig of his fourth long-necked beer and scowled at the poster above his computer. "Enjoyed yourself with Hamilton, did you? I suppose you were planning to tell me you put a bag over his head and thought of Candy Valentine."

He took another long swallow and frowned. "But of course when you found out today that Candy's dead, there was no reason to pretend you did it for the good of the cause. You could tell the truth and shame the devil." Jack stared at Krysta's smiling face. "So ol' Derek's a real studmuffin. Who would have thought a guy with a fake Rolex could get it on?" He raised the bottle in the poster's direction. "Thanks for sharing, Krysta."

His cat jumped into his lap.

"Well, here's a nonpartial observer ready with an opinion. Tell me, cat, can you believe Krysta Lueckenhoff would jump into bed with the likes of Derek Hamilton two days after making mind-blowing love to yours truly?"

The cat meowed and began kneading her claws into the denim of his jeans.

"Well, I can't, either, no matter how mad she was at me. She even told me it was so, told me straight out, and I still can't buy it. Maybe in about fifty years I'll understand what happened."

The cat circled his lap and settled down.

"Oh, and by the way, I've changed your name back to 'cat,'" he muttered, stroking the tabby's golden fur. "Then you and me, we're goin' on a trip, living off the land, like I did before. That's after I tell Mr. Fake Rolex where he can put a very large paper bale, which will likely get my ass fired."

The cat began to purr.

"You like that idea, do you? You'll purr out of the other side of your mouth when we run out of Tender Vittles."

The cat gazed up at him with eyes that were a familiar green.

"And to answer your question, no, you are not going to be a famous author's cat. Not unless I decide to opt for a sex change." He scratched behind the tabby's ears. "Krysta was right. They'd bought the whole package, and now I'm relegated to the bottom of the list. No display dump, no book tour. They were royally ticked at me, cat. Indignant city."

Jack sighed and tipped the bottle back to drain it. Then he lined it up next to the three empties on top of his computer terminal and reached for another. Four down and two to go. The computer screen, gray and lifeless, reflected his grim expression as he unscrewed the cap.

PUTTING ON RAIN GEAR the next morning seemed stupid to Jack when he was on his way to get fired, so he threw on his ski jacket, jumped on his Harley and took off through the downpour for his showdown with Derek Hamilton. Even if Krysta had enjoyed it, Hamilton couldn't get away with asking a woman for sexual favors in exchange for privileges at work. Not if Jack had anything to say about it, and as a matter of fact, he had plenty to say. He arrived in Hamilton's outer office completely soaked.

The secretary eyed him with distaste as he dripped on the carpet. "Do you have an appointment?" she asked.

"Mr. Hamilton and I have had this appointment for months," Jack said. "We just hadn't settled on the exact time."

"Let me check with him." She picked up the receiver on her desk phone. "Your name?"

"I'll announce myself." Jack headed for the closed door of Hamilton's office.

"Just a minute, Mr.—"

Jack ignored her and walked in, locking the door behind him.

Hamilton half rose from behind his desk, his expression startled.

"Hello, there, Derek." Jack approached the desk. "I'm here to talk about Krysta Lueckenhoff."

"Oh." Hamilton seemed to recover himself somewhat. "Don't worry. She's been dismissed."

"She's been *what?*" Jack roared.

Hamilton drew himself up to his full height, which still lacked a few inches to allow him to go eyeball-to-eyeball with Jack. "We can't have that kind of behavior from employees here at Rainier. It was quite embarrassing, really."

"You slimeball. You dangle special company privileges in front of her so she'll sleep with you, and when she does, you *dismiss* her?" Jack reached across the desk and grabbed Hamilton by the tie. "I was going to tell you exactly what I thought of you, and I'm damn good with words, but sometimes words aren't enough." He clenched his fist.

"Sleep with me? Hell, she turned me down!"

"What did you say?"

"She was after you, you numbskull!"

Jack let go of Hamilton's tie. "What do you mean, after me?"

The vice president sank back into his swivel chair and loosened his tie, but kept his gaze riveted on Jack. "You're fired, Killigan."

"Yeah, yeah, I know. Just tell me what you were talking about a minute ago." A warm glow suffused the region of his heart. Maybe she hadn't gone to bed with this bozo, after all.

"I'm sure you know the details far better than I do. She followed you to New York and tried to seduce you. Surely, despite your limited intelligence, you would notice a woman of Krysta's caliber throwing herself at you."

"Who told you she did that?"

"She did, after I confronted her with the fact that you'd both been on the same plane to New York. She confessed that she'd followed you on purpose when she learned of your travel plans. She had a taste for brawn over brains, was the impression I got. We can't have people in the organization who are ruled by their hormones, so I let her go."

Jack folded his arms to keep from reaching for this sorry excuse for a man one more time. "And just when did this little interchange take place, where she confessed and you fired her?"

"This discussion is over, Killigan. You're lucky I haven't called security."

Jack lost the battle to control himself. In one swift movement, he grabbed Hamilton by the front of his white silk shirt and lifted him from the chair. *"When did you fire her?"*

Hamilton turned pale. "Monday night."

"Let's review our conversation." Jack narrowed his gaze as he peered into Hamilton's pale eyes. "Contrary to your opinion of my intelligence, I have an excellent memory for dialogue. Right before I was ready to punch you in the nose, you blurted out that Krysta *turned you down.* Do you happen to remember that statement?"

"You misunderstood."

Jack tightened his grip and lowered his voice. "Wrong. I understood perfectly. You've just admitted to sexually harassing a female employee, then firing her when she wouldn't cooperate." He shoved Hamilton back into his chair. "If Krysta will testify, we have grounds for a lawsuit."

"*We* have grounds? How come you're so chummy all of a sudden? I thought you didn't even like her!"

"What I feel for that woman goes way beyond liking, and it's time I quit wasting my breath on you and told her so." He turned to go.

"You're still fired!" Hamilton shouted.

"Fine with me. I wouldn't want to work for you, anyway." Jack kept walking.

"And I didn't fire her!"

Jack paused and glanced back. "You didn't?"

"No." Hamilton straightened his shirtfront and adjusted his vest. "She quit."

"I don't think that's going to help you much," Jack said. "But you have no idea what it does for me." He left Hamilton's office and took the fire stairs two at a time down to the floor where the contracts office was located. On the way down he let out a yell of jubilation that echoed in tune with his rapid footsteps on the metal stairs.

Rosie glanced up and raised her eyebrows when he burst in. "It's about time."

"Where is she?"

"Home typing up her résumé and nursing a slight hangover. If you hadn't shown up I was going to use my coffee break to come and get you, Mr. Candy Valentine. I was planning to tell your foreman all about this little sideline of yours, and watch you squirm."

"I gather Krysta told you what's been going on."

"She told me enough, after I plied her with some wine, to make me wonder if my first favorable assessment of you was mistaken. You may be the best lover God ever created, but—"

"Did she say that?"

"I'm not telling. I just have one question for you, lov-erboy. Are you going to do right by that woman, or will I have to ask some friends of mine to work you over?"

Jack's smile was grim. "Save your efforts for putting Hamilton away."

"Now, *there's* a cause I could get into. I asked around a little yesterday, and I don't think Krysta's the only one with a complaint."

"That's music to my ears. But Hamilton can wait. I need directions to Krysta's apartment, assuming you're pretty sure she's there right now."

Rosie leaned her chin on her hand and looked up at him. "I'm not giving directions to some guy who's going to use and abuse my good friend and then aban-don her when he finds out he's about to become rich and famous."

Jack groaned. "I would never abandon Krysta. I'm crazy about her."

"How crazy?"

Jack leaned both hands on Rosie's desk and gazed into her brown eyes. "Give me directions to her apart-ment and I'm sure you'll find out the next time you ply her with a bottle of wine."

"Uh-huh." Rosie gazed back at him. "I'm beginning to see what that girl was raving about. You do have a way about you."

"I'm going to marry her, Rosie."

"Oo-wee!" Rosie wiggled her shoulders in delight. "I love stuff like this. Come around the desk and pay attention while Rosie draws you a map, Mr. Valen-tine."

15

IT WAS A TOSS-UP which ached worse, her head or her heart, Krysta thought as she sat in front of her word processor and updated her résumé. The rain pattering against her apartment windows fit her mood perfectly.

Already bored with the morning's assigned job, she decided to amuse herself by typing "Stand-in for Male Romance Author" as her most recent position. Under "Duties" she listed contract negotiation, revision consultant, dinner companion, roommate...lover. With a sigh she hit the delete button. She'd been a good Candy Valentine, dammit. Not everyone could have performed the role as well as she had. Even Rosie had said so.

She probably shouldn't have gone out with Rosie, although it had temporarily eased her distress to talk about her troubles and drink more red wine than was good for her. But this morning there was no Rosie, no wine, no job and definitely no Jack Killigan.

She'd forced herself to shower and dress, despite having no office to go to and no boss to satisfy. For the time being, her dining room table would be her office, and she would be the boss in charge of the great Krysta Lueckenhoff job search. She had a meager savings account that could take her through a few weeks if she scrimped.

She stared at the small screen on her word processor

and longed for the computer she'd used at Rainier. Rosie had offered to put together her résumé for her and run it off on the laser printer in the office, but Krysta hadn't been that sort of employee and she didn't want to become that sort of ex-employee. Despite Rosie's insistence that the company owed her that much, she'd turned down the offer in favor of using her own word processor, limited though it might be.

She heard a motorcycle outside her living room window, and for one wild moment thought maybe...but, no. She'd have to stop imagining the sort of ending to this story that Jack would write in one of his novels. He'd even been the one who'd told her to separate fantasy from reality.

When her doorbell buzzed, she jumped and knocked her chair over. Telling herself it was either the Avon lady or a magazine salesman, she walked toward the door, her heart pounding. Then she squinted through the peephole and her heart threatened to stop altogether.

With a trembling hand she unlocked the door and opened it to the wettest, most magnificent man in the world. "You're soaked, Jack."

He grinned at her and stepped inside. "And you're hung over, Krysta."

She backed up. "And how would you know?"

"Do you deny it?"

"You've been talking to Rosie, haven't you." She backed up some more. He looked too appealing, and she didn't want to fall victim to that magnetism when there was no future in it.

"Among other people." He shortened the distance between them again.

"I'll bet you come down with a bad cold, riding around in the rain like that."

He advanced, his blue gaze intense. "If I do, will you be my nurse?"

"Absolutely not." She retreated farther. "Why aren't you at work?"

"I was fired." He stepped closer.

"Fired? But Jack, your book won't be out until next year! What will you do until then?"

He shrugged. "Something will turn up."

"That is so typical of you." She tried to break eye contact, but the old fascination with Jack remained and she couldn't do it. "I suppose you have no plan whatsoever."

"Oh, I have a plan."

Her blood thrummed through her veins. "You... do?"

"I do. But first I have a few questions. Did you tell Rosie I was the best lover God ever created?"

Heat climbed into her face. Doggone that Rosie. She was supposed to be her friend. "That was the wine talking. In point of fact, I think you're—"

"I'll take it, wine-induced though it might have been. Did you go to bed with Hamilton?"

She opened her mouth to say yes, but the lie wouldn't come out. "No."

A gleam of triumph shone in his eyes. "Then why did you tell me you had?"

"I didn't."

"Oh, yes, you did. I distinctly remember you shoving my nose in the fact and adding that you'd enjoyed it."

"I never told you specifically what I enjoyed." Her

chin lifted. "You jumped to conclusions, and I let you jump. Served you right."

"You're right, it did." His expression gentled. "It would also serve me right if you refused to forgive me for having so little faith in you. But I'll ask, anyway, because I'm a desperate man." He paused. "Please forgive me, Krysta."

When he looked at her like that, all the anger seeped right out of her. "I guess you had your reasons for thinking that way."

"More instincts than reasons. When I thought Hamilton might get the woman I wanted, I turned into a complete jerk."

A quiver ran through her. "The woman you wanted? I don't recall you ever mentioning that you wanted me for more than a weekend in New York."

"Right again. Because I felt I had nothing to offer you."

"Nothing to offer?" All her anger and frustration came rushing back. "You must take me for a fool. You're going to be a bestselling author!"

"I know Manchester's enthusiasm convinced you of that, but I've read hundreds of magazine articles about this business. You *never* know if a book will be a success. You can't count on the income it will bring. It could be fantastic, or it could be a total mirage, and like a mirage, you won't know until you get there."

Under the glamorous spell of that weekend in New York, Krysta hadn't been able to consider such a truth. But today, back home in Evergreen, it seemed more logical to her. Yet she hated to give up the certainty of Jack's stardom so easily. "I still say you're going to be famous."

"Your faith in me is wonderful, but there was no guarantee of that then, and there's even less now."

"What do you mean? They're putting book dumps in the front of stores, and they—" She paused when the meaning behind his statement hit her. Oh, no. "Jack, what's happened?" She was afraid to hear his answer.

He ran a hand through his damp hair and glanced away. "Manchester isn't very happy to discover that a guy wrote those books. Some of the publishing plans are changing."

"But you said—"

"I know what I said. I wasn't completely truthful yesterday because I didn't want you to worry. What's done is done, anyway."

"Oh, Jack! Why on earth did you tell them?"

"Because I thought if I didn't, you were going to risk your career to go on that damned tour. But I was too late."

Her stomach clutched. "You mean that everything we went through has been for nothing?"

His startled gaze met hers. "Nothing?" He gripped her by the arms. "You're calling the most fantastic weekend of our lives *nothing?*"

"I was talking about your publishing career, Jack! That's the important thing right now."

"No, it isn't." He pulled her against his soggy jacket, dampening her blouse. "To hell with my publishing career."

"Don't say that. Don't ever say that."

"It's a free country, Krysta. I'll say whatever I want. I'll even say I love you."

She looked into his eyes and felt as if someone had just knocked the breath from her lungs. "Jack..."

He stepped away from her and caught her by the hand. "Come here," he said, starting toward the door.

She pulled back. "Jack, are you crazy? It's cold. And it's raining out there."

"Precisely." He tugged her through the door and closed it. The storm door slammed after them. Then he pulled her, sputtering and protesting all the way, out into the drizzle.

"Now." He stopped and drew her into his arms.

She shivered in the cold. "I wish you'd tell me what this is all about."

"The first lesson a writer learns is 'show, don't tell.'" He tilted her face up.

"Jack, I'm getting rain in my eyes."

"Then, close them, Krysta," he murmured.

And then she understood. His mouth touched her rain-cooled cheeks, warming them. His tongue followed the path of a droplet to a corner of her mouth. She drank in the rain, drank in the moist caress of his lips, drank in his love.

As happy tears joined the cascade that had become a benediction, she forgot the chill in the air, forgot the cars whizzing by on the street next to the apartment building, forgot the neighbors who might be staring out the window. But she remembered what he'd once said to her. *All I have to offer is a kiss in the rain.* It was more than enough.

He lifted his head and gazed down at her. "I love you, Krysta. I'll do whatever it takes to keep us together. I'll work extra jobs to help pay for your father's care."

"No." She swallowed and blinked back tears. "I won't have you sacrifice your writing for that."

"If I can't be with you, my writing holds no joy for me."

She cradled his face in both hands. "I won't be the burden that keeps you from writing, Jack."

"No, you'll be my inspiration, just as you have been for months." His mouth hovered over hers. "And I really need some inspiration, Krysta." This time his mouth descended with less delicacy and more hunger. His embrace became more urgent, his tongue more demanding.

She managed to wrench her mouth from his. Their hot breath clouded the air as they gazed at each other. "We'd better go inside to continue this discussion," she said, sliding her fingers through his.

"Good idea."

Krysta ran with him up the steps and pulled at the storm door. It was locked. She glanced at him and started to laugh. "We're locked out."

"Let me try." He grasped the handle and pulled hard.

"It's no use. Sometimes the lock just clicks into place by itself. I've told the landlord, but so far he hasn't fixed it."

"I don't suppose you've left any windows open."

"Nope."

"Then there's only one thing left to do." He took off his ski jacket. "Put this on," he commanded, guiding her arms into the sleeves.

"Jack, what about you?"

"You're going to keep me warm. Come on."

Moments later they were on his motorcycle headed along the streets of Evergreen. Krysta wrapped herself tightly around him in an attempt to keep him from freezing to death. She wasn't sure how he was doing, but the friction of their bodies as Jack navigated the turns was keeping her toasty, not to mention extremely aroused. And she'd thought motorcycles were stupid.

At his apartment, he parked the bike and whipped her up the stairs almost at a run. A tabby cat greeted them at the door. "Krysta, my love, meet Krysta, my cat," Jack said.

"You named your cat after me?"

He shrugged. "She has your eyes."

"Oh, really?" Krysta tried to look into the cat's face, but Jack pulled her toward the bedroom.

"Take off your clothes," he said.

"What happened to all that romance you're supposed to be famous for?"

"There's nothing romantic about catching cold together. We're taking a warm shower." He winked. "Now *that* might get very romantic."

It did. Jack's ministrations under the warm spray soon left Krysta too weak to stand. Afterward, he toweled her off, swept her into his arms and carried her to his bed, where he finished what he'd so adequately started.

As they lay sated in each other's arms, he reached over to the bedside table and picked up a small object. "I think you left your heart in New York," he said, handing her the plastic toy he'd bought.

She sighed and took the heart. "I sure did. You don't know how I puzzled over this when you gave it to me. I couldn't decide if it was a clever joke or a real request."

"It was a real request." He pushed the arrow shaft

in, and the *Be My Valentine* message popped up. "Will you?"

She smiled at him. "You're eleven months early."

"I believe in getting a head start. Which reminds me." He took the heart from her and put it back on the bedside table. "I have a new proposal ready."

"You do?" She ran her fingers through his damp hair. "Goodness, Jack. You must have been working night and day to come up with one that fast."

"Actually, this one took longer than it should have, but then, it's the most important proposal of my life, so I guess that's okay."

"Is it a romance?"

His gaze was tender. "You bet it is."

Her breath caught in her throat at the look in his eyes. "We're not talking about a book, are we?"

He shook his head.

Her pulse quickened in anticipation.

"Krysta, I—" He stopped and cleared his throat. "Damn, I want to get this right."

"I don't think you could possibly get it wrong."

"Wanna bet? I may have written these scenes but I've never tried it out in real life." He gave her a sheepish grin. "Okay, here goes." He took a deep breath. "Krysta, will you—"

The phone beside the bed rang and Jack frowned. "Ignore it. The answering machine in the other room will pick it up." He turned back to her as the phone stopped ringing and his voice on the answering machine message filtered in from the living room. He spoke over it. "Krysta, will—"

"Jack, that's Stephanie Briggs on the phone! I recognize her voice!"

"Who cares? I'm in the middle of something very important. I'll call her back later."

"Later?" She extricated herself from his arms and started to climb out of bed. "That's not very wise if you're about to take on the responsibilities of a wife, Jack."

"I didn't even ask you yet!"

She grabbed a towel and wrapped herself in it as she hurried out to the living room. "I'm going to answer that phone. Then you can ask me. And I'll tell you in advance my answer is yes."

"Krysta!" Jack roared.

She ignored him, punched the stop button on the answering machine and picked it up, interrupting Stephanie in midsentence. "Hello? This is Mr. Killigan's personal assistant and I just walked in the door. May I help you?"

"Candy, is that you?"

"Uh, my name is Krysta Lueckenhoff."

"Your name is Candy Valentine," Stephanie said. "Or at least it was a few days ago. I never forget a voice. Listen, you and your friend Jack threw us all for a loop around here, and now I'm in charge of damage control. Obviously I can't send a guy on tour as Candy Valentine."

"Obviously," Krysta agreed. She glanced over her shoulder as Jack came in with a towel draped around his hips.

"Unfortunately, I didn't get a look at your Jack. I should have just opened the closet door, but I, of course, thought he was some hayseed you'd dragged along with you to New York."

"He's no hayseed," Krysta said.

Jack lifted his eyebrows.

"What does he look like? Is he presentable?"

Not at the moment. Krysta stifled a laugh. "If you dressed him right, he'd look pretty good."

Jack scowled at her.

"Is he sexy?"

Krysta gave Jack the once-over. "Definitely."

"How about compared to Fabio?"

"He'd give Fabio a run for his money. He's even been known to wear his hair long."

Jack started forward. "Now, wait just a damn minute. I'm not shaving my chest or—"

Krysta twisted away from him and walked the length of the cord.

"We may be able to salvage this situation yet," Stephanie said. "If he photographs well, we can do a promotion billing him as Jack Killigan—Mr. Valentine."

"I think that sounds like a terrific idea," Krysta said.

"We'll have to fly you both back to New York, I guess. The accountants won't like that, but I'll handle them."

"Both of us?"

"Both of you, Candy. Or Krysta, or whatever your name is. It's obvious you've got a head for the business, and I've enjoyed dealing with you. No telling what I'd run into with Mr. Valentine, there."

Krysta danced out of Jack's reach. "You have a point."

"Okay." Stephanie heaved a big sigh. "I'm rescheduling the twenty-city tour and crossing my fingers."

"I think we can do twenty-five cities."

Jack gaped at her and began waving his hands in the air.

"Is that right?" Stephanie asked. "You're a regular little hustler, aren't you."

"I believe in Jack's talent. He's going to be big."

"Well, fortunately for you, I believe in his talent, too. I'll see about extending the tour. And when I have dates for the return trip to New York, I'll let you know. Are you both at this number?"

Krysta winked at Jack. "We're both at this number."

"Good. He needs you. I'll be in touch."

Krysta hung up the phone and turned to Jack.

He folded his arms across his chest. "Looks like I've been preempted."

"On what?"

"My proposal."

"Oh, Jack, do you really mind?" She crossed to him. "My answer is yes anyway."

"What, no negotiating?"

"What on earth would I negotiate? I love you so much, that I—"

He placed his hands on her shoulders. "Hold it right there."

She paused and glanced up at him.

"Back up that train. What did you just say?"

She ran her palms over his chest and gazed into his eyes. "I love you so much."

He closed his eyes. "Say it again. Slower."

She stood on tiptoe and wound her arms around his neck. "The first rule of writing, according to someone who should know, is 'show, don't tell.'"

With a groan of impatience he pulled her close. "You

can show me in a minute. Tell me now. I need to hear it."

"I love you, Jack. I want to be your wife, your friend, your lover, your business consultant, your personal assistant, your contract negotiator, your—"

"My everything." He gazed down at her and shook his head. "Twenty-five cities?"

"You never know what you can get unless you ask."

"Is that so?" He leaned down and whispered an extremely provocative request.

"Perhaps that can be arranged." She began to unwind the towel from his hips.

"Just promise me one thing."

"Anything, my love."

"That I won't have to shave my chest."

"You won't have to shave your chest," she murmured as her own towel dropped to the floor.

"You're sure?"

"I'm sure." She caressed him intimately. "You're in my hands now, Mr. Valentine."

Heartbreak RANCH

Four generations of independent women…
Four heartwarming, romantic stories of the West…
Four incredible authors…

Fern Michaels
Jill Marie Landis
Dorsey Kelley
Chelley Kitzmiller

Saddle up with Heartbreak Ranch, an outstanding
Western collection that will take you on a whirlwind
trip through four generations and the exciting,
romantic adventures of four strong women who
have inherited the ranch from Bella Duprey,
famed Barbary Coast madam.

Available in March,
wherever Harlequin books are sold.

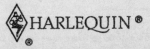

HARLEQUIN ®